ALEXANDER AND NADIA PLUNGED through the vegetation. It seemed to them that they were following a faint path through the forest, maybe a very old trail that had filled in with plants but was still used by animals going to the river to drink.

Suddenly through the unrelenting sounds of the forest they could hear something similar to a human lament, shocking enough to make them stop and listen. Borobá began jumping up and down nervously, indicating that they needed to keep going. Some yards farther on, they saw what was disturbing him. Alexander, who was in the lead, came within a few feet of falling into a pit yawning at his feet, a kind of deep trench. The cry was originating from a dark form that at first sight they took to be a large dog.

"What is it?" murmured Alexander, stepping back and not daring to raise his voice.

The creature in the hole moved, and then they could see it was some kind of simian. It was tangled in a net that had completely immobilized it. The animal looked up and when it saw them began to roar and bare its teeth.

"It's a gorilla," said Nadia. "It can't get out."

ALSO BY ISABEL ALLENDE

Isabel Allende

Forest of the Pygmies

Translated from the Spanish by
MARGARET SAYERS PEDEN

rayo

HarperTrophy®
An Imprint of HarperCollins*Publishers*

For Brother Fernando de la Fuente,
missionary in Africa,
whose spirit animates this story

Rayo is an imprint of HarperCollins Publishers.
Harper Trophy® is a registered trademark
of HarperCollins Publishers.
Forest of the Pygmies
Copyright © 2004 by Isabel Allende

Library of Congress Cataloging-in-Publication Data
Allende, Isabel.
 [Bosque de los Pigmeos. English]
 Forest of the Pygmies / Isabel Allende ; translated from the
Spanish by Margaret Sayers Peden.—1st ed.
  p.   cm.
 Summary: Eighteen-year-old Alexander Cold and his grandmother
travel to Africa on an elephant-led safari, but discover a corrupt world
of poaching and slavery.
 ISBN-10: 0-06-076198-9 — ISBN-13: 978-0-06-076198-1
 [1. Elephants—Fiction. 2. Grandmothers—Fiction.
3. Poaching—Fiction. 4. Kenya—Fiction. 5. Adventure and
adventurers—Fiction.] I. Peden, Margaret Sayers. II. Title.
PZ7.A43912Fo 2005   2004014448
[Fic]—dc22   CIP
                                                   AC

Typography by Hilary Zarycky
❖
First Harper Trophy edition, 2006

Contents

CHAPTER ONE

The Market Fortune-teller

✦

AT AN ORDER FROM THE guide, Michael Mushaha, the elephant caravan came to a stop. The suffocating heat of midday was beginning, when the creatures of the vast nature preserve rested. Life paused for a few hours as the African earth became an inferno of burning lava, and even hyenas and vultures sought the shade. Alexander Cold and Nadia Santos were riding a willful bull elephant named Kobi. The animal had taken a liking to Nadia, because during their time together she had made an effort to learn the basics of the elephant's language in order to communicate with him. During their long treks, she told him about her country, Brazil, a distant land that had no creature as large as he, other than some ancient, legendary beasts hidden deep in the heart of South America's mountains. Kobi appreciated Nadia as much as he detested Alexander, and he never lost an opportunity to demonstrate both sentiments.

Kobi's five tons of muscle and fat shivered to a halt in a small oasis beneath dusty trees kept alive by a pool of water the color of milky tea. Alexander had developed his own style of jumping to the ground from his nine-foot-high perch without mauling himself too badly, since in the five days of their safari he still had not gained the animal's cooperation. He was not aware that this time Kobi had positioned himself in such a way that when Alex jumped down, he landed in a puddle of water up to his knees. Borobá, Nadia's small black monkey, then jumped on top of him. As Alex struggled to pry the monkey off his head, he lost his balance and plopped down on his seat. He cursed to himself, shook off Borobá, and only with difficulty regained his footing because he couldn't see through his glasses, which were dripping filthy water. As he was looking for a clean corner of his T-shirt to wipe the lenses, the elephant thumped him on the back with his trunk, a blow that propelled him face first into the puddle. Kobi waited for Alex to pull himself up, then turned his monumental rear end and unleashed a Pantagruelian blast in his face. The other members of the safari greeted the prank with a chorus of guffaws.

Nadia was in no hurry to get down; she waited for Kobi to help her dismount in a more dignified manner. She stepped upon the knee he offered her, steadied herself on his trunk, and then leaped to the ground with the grace of a ballerina. The elephant was not that considerate with anyone else, not even Mushaha, for whom he had respect but not affection. Kobi was an elephant with clear principles. It was one thing to transport tourists on his back, a job like any other, for which he was rewarded with excellent food and mud baths. It was something entirely different to perform circus tricks for a handful of peanuts. He liked peanuts, he couldn't deny that, but he received much more pleasure from tormenting people like Alexander. Why did the American get under his skin? The animal wasn't sure, it was a matter of chemistry. He didn't like the fact that Alex was always hanging around Nadia. There were thirteen elephants in the caravan, but he had to ride with the girl. It was very inconsiderate of Alex to get between Nadia and him that way. Didn't he realize that they needed privacy for their conversations? A good whack with the trunk and occasionally breaking wind in Alex's face were just what that young man deserved. Kobi trumpeted loudly once Nadia was down and had thanked him by planting a big kiss on his trunk. The girl had good manners; she would never humiliate him by offering him peanuts.

"That elephant is infatuated with Nadia," joked Alexander's grandmother, Kate Cold.

Borobá didn't like the turn Kobi's relationship with his mistress had taken. He had observed them with some worry. Nadia's interest in learning the language of the pachyderms could have dangerous consequences for him. She couldn't be thinking of getting a different pet, could she? Perhaps the moment had come for him to feign some illness in order to gain his mistress's total attention, but he was afraid she would leave him in camp and he would miss the wonderful outings around the preserve. This was his only chance to see the wild animals and, in addition, he wanted to keep a close eye on his rival. He installed himself on Nadia's shoulder, claiming that position as his right, and from there shook his fist at the elephant.

"And this silly monkey is jealous," Kate added.

She was used to Borobá's shift of moods, because she had lived under the same roof with him for nearly two years. It was like having a freakish, furry little man in her apartment. And it had been that way from the beginning, because Nadia had agreed to come to New York to study and live with Kate only if she could bring Borobá. They were never apart. They were so inseparable that they had obtained special permission for the monkey to go to school with her. Borobá was the only monkey in the history of the city's education system to attend classes regularly. It wouldn't have surprised Kate to learn that the creature knew how to read. She had nightmares in which Borobá, sitting on the sofa wearing glasses and sipping a glass of brandy, was reading the financial section of the *Times*.

Kate had observed the strange trio formed of Alexander, Nadia, and Borobá for some time. The monkey, who was jealous of anyone who came too near his mistress, had at first accepted Alexander as an inevitable evil, but with time had become fond of the young man. Perhaps he realized that in this instance it was not a good idea for him to offer Nadia the ultimatum of "it's him or me," as he usually did. Who knows which of the two she would have chosen? Kate realized that both young people had changed a lot during the past year. Nadia would soon be fifteen and her grandson eighteen; they already had the physical appearance and seriousness of adults.

Nadia and Alexander were themselves aware of the changes. During their forced separation, they communicated by e-mail with demented persistence. They whiled their lives away in front of their computers, typing an endless dialogue in which they shared everything from the most boring details of their routines to philosophical questions regarding the torment of growing up. They frequently sent photographs, but that had not prepared them for the surprise they experienced when they saw each other in the flesh and verified how much they had grown. Alexander had shot up like a colt, and now was as tall as his father. His features had become well defined, and during recent months he had had to shave every day. As for Nadia, she was no longer the thin little creature with parrot feathers tucked behind one ear whom Alexander had met in the Amazon some years before; he could glimpse the woman she would soon become.

So now the grandmother and the two young people were in the heart of Africa, on the first elephant safari ever conceived for tourists in this region. The idea of the safari was the brainchild of Michael Mushaha, an African naturalist who had graduated from a London university. It had occurred to him that elephants would be the best conveyance for humans who wanted to get as close as possible to the wildlife of the area. In his publicity brochure, he explained: "The elephants are part of the surroundings, and their presence does not drive away the other beasts; they do not need gasoline or a road, they do not pollute the air, and they do not attract attention."

Alexander and Nadia had been with Kate in

Tunkhala, the capital of the Kingdom of the Golden Dragon, when she was commissioned to write an article on Mushaha's operation. They were there at the invitation of King Dil Bahadur and his wife, Pema, to celebrate the birth of their first son and to attend the inauguration of a new statue of the dragon. The original, which had been destroyed in an explosion, had been replaced by an identical copy fashioned by a jeweler friend of Kate's.

For the first time, the people of this Himalayan kingdom had an opportunity to see the mysterious object of legend that in the past only the crowned monarch was privileged to view. Dil Bahadur had decided to exhibit the statue of gold and precious stones in a large hall in the royal palace, where people could file through to admire it and leave their offerings of flowers and incense. It was a magnificent spectacle. The dragon was mounted on a base of polychrome wood and lighted by a hundred lamps. Guarding the statue were four soldiers outfitted in the dress uniform of past centuries: plumed leather hats and token lances. Dil Bahadur would not allow his people to be offended by a show of security measures.

The official unveiling of the statue had just ended when Kate was advised that there was a call for her from the United States. The telephone system of the kingdom was antiquated, and international communications were a nightmare, but after much shouting and repetition, the editor of *International Geographic* was successful in making the writer understand the nature of her next assignment. She was to leave immediately for Africa.

"I will have to take my grandson and his friend Nadia; they're here with me," she explained.

"The magazine is not paying their expenses, Kate!" the editor yelled.

"Then I'm not going!" she screamed in return.

And so it was that a few days later she arrived in Africa with Alexander and Nadia. There they were joined by the two photographers who always worked with her, the Englishman Timothy Bruce and the Latin American Joel González. The writer had promised herself never to travel again with her grandson and Nadia because they had caused her so much trouble on their two earlier trips. She felt sure, however, that a simple sojourn for tourists in Africa would not present any danger.

One of Mushaha's employees met the members of the group when they landed in Nairobi, the capital of

Kenya. He welcomed them and took them to a hotel to rest, because the trip had been a killer: They had taken four airplanes, crossed three continents, and flown thousands of miles.

The next morning they got up early in order to take a tour of the city and visit a museum and the market before setting off in the small airplane that would take them to the start of the safari.

The market was in a poor neighborhood surrounded by luxuriant vegetation. The narrow, unpaved streets were choked with people and vehicles: motorcycles carrying three and four people, broken-down buses, hand-pulled carts. A vast variety of the produce of earth and sea, and of human creativity, was for sale there, from rhinoceros horns and golden fish from the Nile to contraband weapons. The members of the group went different ways, after agreeing to meet one hour later at a predetermined street corner. That would be easier to say than do, because there was such tumult and uproar that it would be difficult to get their bearings. Fearing that Nadia would get lost or be run down, Alexander took her by the hand and they went off together.

The market was a showcase of African races and cultures: desert nomads; slender horsemen on elegantly outfitted steeds; Muslims with elaborate turbans and partially veiled faces; women with burning eyes and blue designs tattooed on their faces; naked shepherds, their bodies painted with red clay and white chalk. Hundreds of children raced barefoot among roaming packs of dogs. The women were spectacular. Some were wearing dazzling starched kerchiefs on their heads that from a distance resembled the sails of a ship; others' heads were shaved clean and bead collars covered their necks from shoulder to chin; some were enveloped in yards and yards of brilliantly patterned cloth, while still others were nearly naked. The air was filled with incessant jabbering in several languages, along with music, laughter, horns, and the cries of animals being slaughtered on the spot. Blood streamed from the butchers' tables, soaking into the dusty ground, while black buzzards circled close overhead, waiting to seize the discarded guts.

Alexander and Nadia wandered through that fiesta of color, marveling, pausing to bargain over the price of a glass bracelet, savor a corn cake, or snap a photo with the cheap camera they had bought at the last moment in the airport. Suddenly they were nose to nose with an ostrich restrained by a rope around one foot, unknowingly awaiting its fate. The bird, much taller, stronger, and more aggressive than they could have imagined, observed them from on high with infinite disdain, and then, without warning, bent its long neck and pecked at Borobá, who was riding atop Alexander's head and clinging firmly to his ears. The monkey twisted away to avoid the lethal beak and began screeching as if he were crazed. The ostrich, beating its short wings, charged at them as far as the rope would allow. By chance, Joel happened along at that very moment and captured the frightened expressions of Alexander and the monkey as Nadia waved her arms to fend off the unexpected attacker.

"This photograph is going to make the cover of *International Geographic!*" Joel shouted.

Fleeing from the haughty ostrich, Nadia and Alexander rounded a corner and suddenly found themselves in a section of the market devoted to witchcraft. There were practitioners of good magic and bad magic—fortune-tellers, fetishists, healers, poison brewers, exorcists, voodoo priests—all offering their services to clients under squares of canvas stretched on four poles for protection from the sun. They came from many tribes and belonged to an assortment of cults. Never dropping each other's hands, the two friends wandered the alleyways, pausing before tiny animals in jars of alcohol; desiccated reptiles; amulets to protect against the evil eye and love sickness; medicinal herbs, lotions, and balms to cure ills of body and soul; powders for dreams, for forgetting, for restoring life; live animals for sacrifices; necklaces to drive away envy and greed; inks made from blood for writing to the dead; and, last but not least, an enormous array of exotic items to mitigate the terror of life.

Nadia had seen voodoo ceremonies in Brazil, and she was more or less familiar with their symbols, but for Alexander this area of the market was a fascinating world. They stopped before one stand different from the others: a conical straw roof that supported a circle of plastic curtains. Alexander bent down to see what was inside, and two powerful hands grabbed him and pulled him into the hut.

An enormous woman was seated on the ground beneath the straw ceiling, a mountain of flesh crowned by a voluminous turquoise kerchief. She was dressed in yellow and blue, and her bosom was covered with necklaces of many-colored beads. She introduced herself as a messenger between the world of the spirits and the material world, a seer and voodoo priestess. On the ground beside her was a cloth painted with designs in black and white. She was surrounded by various carved wood figures of gods and demons, some wet with the fresh blood of sacrificed animals, others studded with nails, and before them lay offerings of fruits, grains, flowers, and money. The woman was puffing on some black leaves rolled into a tight cylinder, and the thick smoke brought tears to the young people's eyes. Alexander tried to free himself from the hands that had immobilized him, but the woman fixed her bulging eyes on him and let out a deep roar. Alexander recognized the voice of his totemic animal, the voice he heard when he was in a trance and his body took on a different form.

"It's the black jaguar!" Nadia exclaimed at his side.

The priestess forced the American boy to sit before her. She pulled a worn leather sack from her bosom and emptied its contents onto the painted cloth: white shells, worn smooth with wear. She began to mutter something in her language, without relinquishing the cigar, which she held clamped between her teeth.

"*Anglais?* English?" Alexander queried.

"You come from a distant place, far away. What do you want of Má Bangesé?" she replied in a comprehensible mixture of African words and English.

Alexander shrugged his shoulders and smiled

nervously, looking at Nadia out of the corner of his eye to see if she had any idea what was going on. She pulled a couple of bills from her pocket and put them in one of the gourds that held the offerings of money.

"Má Bangesé can read your heart," said the gigantic woman, speaking to Alexander.

"And what is in my heart?"

"You are looking for medicines to cure a woman," she said.

"My mother isn't sick any longer; her cancer is in remission . . ." Alexander murmured, frightened, not understanding how a witch in a market in Africa could know about Lisa Cold.

"At any rate, you fear for her," said Má Bangesé. She shook the shells in one hand and tossed them like dice. "The life or death of that woman is not in your hands," she added.

"Will she live?" Alexander asked anxiously.

"If you go back, she will live. If you do not, she will die of sadness, not illness."

"Of course I'm going back home!" the youth protested.

"Nothing is sure. There is much danger, but you are strong of heart. You must use your courage, otherwise you will die and this girl will die with you," she declared, pointing to Nadia.

"What does that mean?" Alexander asked.

"A person can do harm, and a person can do good. There is no reward for doing good, only satisfaction in your soul. There are times you must fight. You will have to decide."

"What am I to do?"

"Má Bangesé sees the heart; she cannot show the way."

And turning toward Nadia, who had sat down beside Alexander, she placed a finger on her forehead, between her eyes.

"You are magic, and you have the vision of birds; you see from above, from afar. You can help him," she said.

She closed her eyes and began to rock back and forth as sweat poured down her face and neck. The heat was unbearable. The smells of the market filled their nostrils: rotted fruit, garbage, blood, gasoline. Má Bangesé let forth a guttural sound that came from deep in her belly, a long, hoarse lament that rose in tone until the ground shook, as if it came from the depths of the earth. Dizzy and perspiring, Nadia and Alexander were afraid they were going to faint. The air in the tiny, smoke-filled space became unbreathable. More and more befuddled, they wanted to leave but they couldn't move. They were shaken by the vibration of drums; they heard dogs howling, their mouths filled with bitter saliva, and before their incredulous eyes the enormous woman melted away, like a burst balloon, and in her place emerged a fabulous bird with splendid yellow and blue plumage and a turquoise-colored crest. This bird-of-paradise unfolded the rainbow of its wings, wrapped Nadia and Alex inside, and flew away with them.

Nadia and Alexander were launched into space. They could see themselves like two pinpoints of black ink lost in a kaleidoscope of brilliant colors and undulating forms mutating at a terrifying speed. They were transformed into Roman candles, their bodies exploding into sparks. They lost any notion of being alive, or of time or fear. Then the sparks fused into an electric vortex, and again they saw themselves as two minute points caroming among the designs of the fantastic kaleidoscope. Now they were two astronauts, hand in hand, floating in starry space. They could not feel their bodies but they had a vague awareness of movement and of being connected. They clung to that contact, because it was the one manifestation of their humanity; as long as they were holding hands they were not totally lost.

Green, they were immersed in total greenness. They

began to plunge earthward like arrows, and when impact seemed inevitable, the color diffused, and instead of crashing they floated down like feathers, sinking into surreal vegetation, into the warm, moist, cottony flora of another planet. Dissolving in the mists of that atmosphere, they metamorphosed into transparent medusas. In that gelatinous state, lacking bones to give them form, or strength to defend themselves, or voices to call out, they confronted the violent images passing in rapid succession before them—visions of death, blood, war, and a destroyed forest. A procession of ghosts in chains marched before them, dragging their feet among the carcasses of large animals. They saw baskets filled with human hands, and children and women in cages.

Suddenly they were once again themselves, in their familiar bodies, and then before them, emerging with the terrifying clarity of the worst nightmares, they saw a threatening three-headed ogre, a giant with the skin of a crocodile. The heads were different: One had four horns and the shaggy mane of a lion; the second had no eyes, was bald, and breathed fire through its nostrils; the third had the skull of a leopard, with bloody teeth and the blazing pupils of a demon. All three had gaping jaws and iguana tongues. The monster clumsily thrust its colossal paws at them, trying to claw them.

Its hypnotic eyes bored into them, its three muzzles spewed a thick, poisonous saliva. Again and again Alex and Nadia eluded the ferocious jabs, unable to flee, feeling as if they were mired in a swamp. They evaded the monster for a time that seemed infinite, until suddenly they found they held spears in their hands and they began blindly, desperately, to defend themselves. When they subdued one of the heads, the other two came at them, and if they succeeded in driving back those two, the first returned to the attack. Their weapons broke in the struggle. Then at the final instant, when they were sure to be devoured, they made a superhuman effort and turned into their totemic animals—Alexander into a jaguar and Nadia an eagle—but before that formidable enemy, the ferocity of the first and the wings of the second were impotent . . . Their cries were lost in the bellowing of the ogre.

"Nadia! Alexander!"

The voice of Kate Cold brought them back to the known world, and they found themselves sitting exactly as they had been when their hallucinatory voyage began: in the market in Africa, beneath the straw roof, facing an enormous woman dressed in yellow and blue.

"We heard you yelling. Who is this woman? What happened?" Alexander's grandmother asked.

"It's nothing, Kate. Nothing at all," Alexander managed to get out, his head reeling.

He didn't know how to explain to his grandmother what he had just experienced. Má Bangesé's deep voice seemed to reach them from the dimension of their dreams.

"Stay on your guard," the seer warned them.

"What happened to you?" Kate repeated.

"We saw a monster with three heads. It was invincible . . ." Nadia murmured, still dazed.

"Stay close to each other. Together you can save yourselves; separated you will die," said Má Bangesé.

The next morning the *International Geographic* group flew in a small plane to the vast nature preserve where Michael Mushaha and his elephant safari awaited them. Alexander and Nadia were still feeling the impact of their experience in the market. Alexander concluded that the rolled leaves the sorceress was smoking contained a drug, but that did not explain the fact that Nadia and he had had identical visions. Nadia did not try to rationalize what had happened; for her that terrible voyage was a source of information, a way of learning, as one learns from dreams. The images were sharp in her memory; she was sure that at some moment she would have to call upon them.

The plane was piloted by its owner, Angie Ninderera, an adventuresome woman overflowing with contagious energy, who expanded on their flight plan to make a couple of detours and show them the majestic beauty of the landscape. One hour later they landed in an open field a couple of miles from Mushaha's camp.

Kate was disenchanted with the modern facilities of the safari; she had expected something more rustic. Several pleasant and efficient African guides wearing khaki uniforms and carrying walkie-talkies attended the tourists and looked after the elephants. There were several tents, as large as hotel suites, and a pair of light wood constructions that housed the common areas and kitchens. The beds were hung with white mosquito netting, the furniture was bamboo, and zebra and antelope skins served as rugs. The bathhouses had chemical latrines and ingenious warm-water showers. The camp had an electric generator that operated from seven to ten at night; the rest of the time they managed with candles and oil lamps. The food, prepared by two cooks, was so tasty that even Alexander, who on principle rejected any dish whose name he couldn't spell, devoured it. As a whole, the camp was much more elegant than most of the places Kate had stayed during her years as a professional traveler and writer. She decided that such luxuries detracted from the safari;

she would not forget to criticize them in her article.

In order to take advantage of the coolest hours of the day, the wake-up bell rang at 5:45 A.M., though earlier, with the first ray of sun, they had awakened to the unmistakable sound of colonies of bats returning after flying the entire night. The aroma of fresh-brewed coffee was already on the air. The visitors opened their tents and stepped out to stretch their limbs as the incomparable African sun, a magnificent circle of fire that spanned the horizon, began to rise. The landscape shimmered in the dawn light; it seemed that at any moment the earth, enveloped in a rosy mist, would fade and disappear like a mirage.

Soon the camp was boiling with activity. The cooks called the party to the table, and Mushaha issued his first instructions. After breakfast they would meet for a brief lecture about the animals, birds, and vegetation they would be seeing that day. Timothy and Joel readied their cameras and the employees brought the elephants, which were accompanied by a two-year-old calf that trotted happily alongside its mother. Occasionally the baby needed to be retrieved because it had stopped to puff at butterflies or roll in the mud near waterholes and rivers.

From atop the elephants, the panorama was magnificent. The great beasts moved silently, blending into the landscape. They advanced effortlessly and with massive calm; they also covered many miles in very little time. None of them, other than the calf, had been born in captivity; they were wild animals, and as such unpredictable. Mushaha warned his party that they must follow his directions closely, or he would not be able to guarantee their safety. The only person who tended to violate that rule was Nadia, who from the first day established such a special relationship with the elephants that the director of the safari simply decided to look the other way.

The visitors spent the morning roaming around the preserve. They communicated with gestures, never speaking, so they would not be detected by other animals. Mushaha took the lead, riding the oldest bull of the herd; behind him came Kate and the photographers on females, one of them the mother of the calf; then Alexander, Nadia, and Borobá on Kobi. A pair of safari employees riding young males brought up the rear, carrying provisions: canopies for the siesta, and some of the photographic equipment. They also carried a powerful tranquilizer they could shoot in case they came face-to-face with an aggressive beast.

The pachyderms occasionally stopped to eat leaves from trees where only a few moments before a family of lions had been resting. Other times they passed so near rhinoceroses that Alexander and Nadia could see themselves reflected in a round eye studying them suspiciously from below. The herds of buffaloes and impalas were not spooked by their passing; they may have picked up the odor of the humans, but the powerful presence of the elephants disoriented them. The party was able to amble among timid zebras, photograph at close range a pack of hyenas quarreling over the corpse of an antelope, and stroke the neck of a giraffe as it licked their hands and gazed at them with princess eyes.

"In a few years," Mushaha lamented, "there will be no wild animals in Africa; you will see animals only in parks and reserves."

At noon they stopped beneath protective trees, lunched from the contents of some baskets, and rested in the shade until four or five in the evening. At the hour of siesta, even wild animals lay down to rest, and the broad plain of the preserve lay motionless beneath the burning rays. Mushaha knew the terrain, and he was expert in calculating time and distance, so just as the enormous disk of the sun began to sink below the horizon, they sighted smoke from their camp. Sometimes at night they went out again to watch the animals that came to the river to drink.

CHAPTER TWO

Elephant Safari

❖

ON THE EVENING OF THE third day they had to use the tranquilizers to subdue a group of drunken bandits. Mushaha and his guests were heading back to camp when they received a call that there was an emergency. Shortly afterward a staff member came rolling up in a Land Rover to take them back, leaving the elephants in the care of their keepers. At the camp they found a startling scene. In their absence a band of a half dozen mandrills had been busy demolishing the encampment. Tents lay on the ground and flour, manioc, rice, beans, and canned preserves were strewn everywhere; shredded sleeping bags hung from tree limbs, and chairs and broken tables were piled in the courtyard. The effect was that of a camp swept by a typhoon. The mandrills, headed by one more aggressive than the others, had grabbed pots and pans and were using them as weapons to club one another and to attack anyone who attempted to approach them.

"What's got into them?" exclaimed Mushaha.

"I'm afraid they're a little drunk," suggested one of the guards.

The baboons always hung around the camp, ready to steal anything they could stuff into their mouths. At night they dug through the garbage, and if provisions were not secured, they stole them. They won no points for charm—typically they showed their teeth and growled—but they had respect for humans and kept a prudent distance. This assault was out of the ordinary.

Given the impossibility of overcoming them, Mushaha gave the order to get the tranquilizer guns, but hitting the target was not easy because the mandrills were running and leaping as if possessed. Finally, one by one, the tranquilizer darts hit their marks and the baboons dropped in their tracks. Alexander and Timothy helped pick them up by ankles and wrists and haul them two hundred yards away from the camp, where they snored unmolested until the effects of the drug passed. Their hairy, foul-smelling bodies weighed much more than one would have expected from their size. Alexander, Timothy, and the employees who touched them had to shower, wash their clothing, and dust themselves with insecticide to get rid of the fleas.

As the personnel of the safari labored to restore some order to the chaos, Mushaha discovered the source of the trouble. Through carelessness on the part of the staff, the mandrills had got into Kate and Nadia's tent and found the former's stash of vodka. They had smelled the alcohol from a distance, even though the bottles were sealed. The lead baboon stole a bottle, broke the neck, and shared the contents with its buddies. With the second swallow they were intoxicated, and with the third they fell on the camp like a horde of pirates.

"I need the vodka to ease my bones," Kate complained, realizing that she would have to guard the few bottles she had like gold.

"Doesn't aspirin help?" queried Mushaha.

"Pills are poison! I use nothing but natural products," the writer exclaimed.

Once the mandrills had been quieted and the camp reorganized, someone noticed that Timothy had blood on his T-shirt. With his traditional indifference, the Englishman admitted that he had been bitten.

"It seems that one of those fellows was not completely out," he said in way of explanation.

"Let me see it," Mushaha demanded.

Timothy lifted his left eyebrow. That was the only gesture ever seen on his horse face, and he used it to express any of the three emotions he was capable of feeling: surprise, doubt, and annoyance. In this instance it was the last; he detested any kind of bother, but Mushaha insisted, and he had no choice but to roll up his sleeve. The bite wasn't bleeding any longer, and there were dried scabs at the points where teeth had perforated the skin, but his forearm was swollen.

"These monkeys carry a number of diseases. I am going to give you an antibiotic, but it will be best if you see a doctor," Mushaha announced.

Timothy's left eyebrow rose halfway up his forehead: definitively too much bother.

Mushaha contacted Angie Ninderera by radio and explained the situation. The young pilot replied that she couldn't fly at night, but that she would be there early the next day to pick up Timothy and fly him to Nairobi. The director of the safari could not help but smile: The mandrill's bite would give him an unexpected opportunity to see Angie, for whom he harbored an unconfessed weakness.

Soon Timothy was shivering with fever. Mushaha wasn't sure whether it was because of the wound or a sudden attack of malaria, but in either case he was worried, since the well-being of the tourists was his responsibility.

A group of Masai nomads who often crossed through the preserve had arrived in camp, driving a herd of cattle with long horns. The people were very tall, slim, handsome, and arrogant. They bedecked themselves with intricate bead necklaces and head-bands; the cloth of their skirts was fastened at their waists, and they had spears in their hands. They believed they were the chosen people of God; the land and all it contained belonged to them by divine grace. That gave them the right to appropriate any livestock they saw, a habit that was not well received among the other tribes. Since Mushaha had no cattle, there was nothing to steal from him. His agreement with them was clear: He offered them hospitality when they passed through the park and in return they never touched a hair on the wild animals.

As always, Mushaha offered them food and invited them to stay. The tribe wasn't pleased with the company of the foreigners, but they accepted because one of their children was ill. They were waiting for a healer, who was on her way there to treat the boy. The woman was famous throughout the region; she traveled miles and miles to heal her patients with herbs and the strength of faith. The tribe had no way to communicate with her by modern means, but somehow they had learned that she would come that night, which was why they were willing to stay in Mushaha's domain.

And precisely as they had predicted, when the sun was about to set they heard the distant tinkling of the healer's little bells and amulets.

A wretched, barefoot figure emerged from the red dust of early evening. She was wearing nothing but a short skirt of rags, and her paraphernalia consisted of gourds, medicines, pouches of amulets, and two magical sticks topped with feathers. Her hair, which had never been cut, was divided into long dreadlocks coated with red mud. She looked ancient—her skin hung from her bones in folds—but she stood erect, and her arms and legs were strong. The patient's treatment was carried out only a few yards away from the camp.

"The healer says that the spirit of an offended ancestor has entered the child. She must identify it and send it back to the other world, where it belongs," Mushaha explained.

Joel laughed; he found the idea that something like that could happen in the twenty-first century very amusing.

"Don't laugh, fellow. In eighty percent of the cases, the patient gets well," Mushaha told him.

He added that on one occasion he had seen two people writhing on the ground, biting, foaming at the mouth, groaning, and barking. According to what their families said, they had been possessed by hyenas. This same healer had cured them.

"That's called hysteria," Joel alleged.

Mushaha smiled. "Call it what you want, the fact is that after the ceremony they got well. Western medicine, with all its drugs and electric shocks, rarely gets results that good and that fast."

"Come on, Michael! You're a scientist educated in London, don't tell me that—"

"First of all I'm African," the naturalist interrupted. "In Africa, physicians have realized that instead of ridiculing healers, they should try to work with them. Sometimes the magic gives better results than imported methods. People believe in it, and that's why it works. Suggestion can work miracles. Don't sell our witches short."

Kate got out her pad to make notes on the ceremony, and Joel, ashamed that he had laughed, readied his camera to photograph it.

They placed the naked boy on a blanket on the ground, surrounded by the many members of his family. The old woman began to beat her magic sticks and shake her gourds, dancing in circles and chanting, and soon the tribe joined in. After a while she fell into a trance; her body shook and her eyes rolled back. As that happened, the child on the ground grew rigid; his back arched until only his head and heels supported his body.

The energy of the ceremony shot through Nadia like an electric current, and without thinking, propelled by an unfamiliar emotion, she joined the nomads' chanting and frenetic dancing. The healing lasted several hours, during which, as Mushaha explained, the aged witch absorbed into her own body the evil spirit that had taken possession of the boy. Finally the small patient's rigidity relaxed and he began to cry, which everyone interpreted as a sign of health. His mother took him in her arms and began to rock and kiss him, to the joy of all present.

After about twenty minutes, the healer herself emerged from her trance and announced that the patient was purged of evil and from that very night would be able to eat normally; however, his parents must fast for three days in order to placate the expelled spirit. As her only food and reward, the old woman accepted a gourd containing a mixture of sour milk and fresh blood, which the Masai herdsmen had obtained by making a small cut in the neck of one of the cattle. Then she retired to rest before undertaking the second phase of her labor: drawing out the spirit, which now was inside her, and speeding it to the Great Beyond, where it belonged. The tribe, grateful, moved on farther to spend the night.

"If the system is so effective, we should ask that woman to treat Timothy," Alexander suggested.

"It doesn't work unless you believe," Mushaha replied. "And besides, the healer is exhausted; she has to build up her strength before she can help another patient."

So the English photographer continued to shiver with fever for the rest of the night, while under the stars the little African boy enjoyed his first meal in a week.

Angie Ninderera showed up the next day as she had promised Mushaha in her radio communication. When they saw her plane in the air, they set off in the Land Rover to the landing field to pick her up. Joel wanted to accompany his friend Timothy to the hospital, but Kate reminded him that someone had to take the photographs for the magazine article.

As Mushaha's employees were gassing up the plane and looking after the patient and his luggage, Angie sat down under a tent to rest and enjoy a cup of coffee. She was a brown-skinned African woman, healthy, tall, strong, and always laughing. Her age was anyone's guess; she could be anywhere between twenty-five and forty. Her easy laugh and fresh beauty captivated people from the first moment they saw her. She told them that she was born in Botswana and had learned to pilot planes in Cuba, while she was there on a fellowship. Shortly before he died, her father had sold his ranch and cattle in order to provide her with a dowry, but instead of using the capital to snag a respectable husband as her father wished, she had used it to buy her first airplane. Angie was an uncaged bird that had never built a nest anywhere. Her work took her all over; one day she flew vaccines to Zaire, the next she carried actors and technicians making an action film on the highlands of the Serengeti, or ferried a group of daring mountain climbers to the foot of the legendary Mt. Kilimanjaro. She boasted that she was strong as a buffalo, and to prove it she armwrestled any man willing to accept her challenge and ante up his bet. She had been born with a star-shaped birthmark on her back—according to Angie, a sure sign of good luck. Thanks to that star, she had survived a number of adventures. Once she was on the verge of being stoned to death by a mob in the Sudan; another time she had wandered in a desert in Ethiopia for five days, lost, alone, on foot, with no food and only one bottle of water. But nothing compared to the time that she'd had to parachute from her plane and landed in a crocodile-infested river.

"That was before I had my Cessna Caravan," she hastened to clarify when she told that story to her *International Geographic* clients. "It never fails."

"And how did you get out of that alive?" asked Alexander.

"The crocodiles were kept busy snapping at the chute, and that gave me time to swim to shore and get myself out of there. I made it that time, but sooner or later I'm going to be eaten by crocodiles. It's my destiny."

"How do you know?" Nadia inquired.

"Because that's what I was told by a fortune-teller who could read the future. Má Bangesé has a reputation for never being wrong," Angie replied.

"Má Bangesé? The fat woman who has a stand in the market?" interrupted Alexander.

"That's the one. And she isn't fat, she's . . . robust," clarified Angie, who was sensitive on the matter of weight.

Alexander and Nadia looked at each other, surprised at the strange coincidence.

Despite her considerable girth and her rather brusque manner, Angie was very coquettish. She wore flowered tunics and draped herself in heavy ethnic jewelry she bought at craft fairs, and her lips were always painted bright pink. Her hair was combed into elaborate cornrows studded with colored beads. She said that her line of work was lethal to a woman's hands, and she wasn't about to let hers look like a mechanic's. Her fingernails were long and brightly painted, and to protect her skin she rubbed on turtle fat, which she considered miraculous. The fact that turtles are pretty wrinkled did not diminish her confidence in the product.

"I know several men who're in love with Angie," commented Mushaha, but he refrained from adding that he was one of them.

Angie winked and explained that she would never marry because she had a broken heart. She had fallen in love only once in her life, and that was with a Masai warrior who had five wives and nineteen children.

"He had long bones and amber-colored eyes," she said.

"And what happened?" Nadia and Alexander asked in unison.

"He didn't want to marry me," she concluded with a tragic sigh.

Mushaha laughed. "What a stupid man!"

"I was ten years older and thirty pounds heavier than he was," Angie explained.

The pilot finished her coffee and got ready to leave. All his friends made their farewells to Timothy, whom the previous night's fever had so weakened that he could not even find the strength to lift his left eyebrow.

The last days of the safari raced by very quickly amid the pleasure of the elephant excursions. They ran into the small nomadic tribe again and saw for themselves that the young boy was cured. At the same time, they learned by radio that Timothy was being kept in the hospital with a combination of malaria and an infected mandrill bite that was resistant to antibiotics.

Three days after taking Timothy, Angie returned for them; she stayed that night in the camp so they could leave early the next morning. From the moment they met, she and Kate had struck up a strong friendship: Both were hearty drinkers—beer for Angie and vodka for Kate—and both had a well-stocked arsenal of rip-roaring stories to enthrall their audiences. That night when the group was sitting in a circle around a bonfire, feasting on roast antelope and other delicacies the cooks had prepared, the two women held a verbal tourney to see who was the best at bedazzling listeners with her adventures. Even Borobá was listening to their tales with interest. The little monkey had been dividing his time between hanging around with the humans, whose company he was accustomed to, watching Kobi, and playing with a family of three pygmy chimpanzees Mushaha had adopted.

"They're twenty percent smaller and much more peaceful than normal chimps," Mushaha explained. "The females take the lead in that society. Which means that the pygmy chimps have a better life; there's less competition and more cooperation; they eat and sleep well in their community; and the babies are protected . . . In short, they live a carefree life. Not like other groups of monkeys, in which the males form gangs and do nothing but fight all the time."

"I wish that's how it was with humans!" Kate sighed.

"Those little creatures are a lot like us: We share most of our genetic material with them; even their brain is similar to ours. We obviously have a common ancestor," said Mushaha.

"Then there's hope that someday we may evolve like them," added Kate.

Angie smoked cigarettes that according to her were her only luxury, and she took pride in the fact that her plane smelled of smoke. "Anyone who doesn't like the odor of tobacco can walk," she always told clients who complained. As a reformed smoker, Kate followed the hand of her new friend with avid eyes. She had stopped smoking over a year ago, but the desire was still there, and as she watched the cigarette moving back and forth to Angie's lips, she wanted to weep. She pulled out her empty pipe, which she always had in her pocket for such desperate moments, and chewed on it sadly. She had to admit that the tubercular cough that had made it so hard for her to breathe had gone away. She attributed that to her vodka-spiked tea and the powders that Walimai, Nadia's shaman friend in the Amazon, had given her. Her grandson, Alexander, gave credit for the miracle to an amulet of petrified dragon excrement that had been a gift from Dil Bahadur, who was now king of the Kingdom of the Golden Dragon; he was convinced of its magical properties.

Kate didn't know what to think of her grandson, who once had been extremely rational but now was given to fantasies. His friendship with Nadia had changed him. Alex had such confidence in that fossil that he had finely ground a few grams to powder, dissolved that in rice liquor, and insisted that his mother drink the potion to fight her cancer. Lisa, his mother, also had worn what was left of the fossil around her neck for months, and now it was around Alexander's, who didn't take it off even to shower.

"It can cure broken bones and lots of other things, Kate, and it wards off arrows, knives, and bullets," her grandson had assured her.

"In your place I wouldn't have put it to the test," she replied dryly, but she had allowed him to rub her chest and back with the artifact, growling all the time that they were both losing their minds.

That last night around the campfire, Kate and the others of her party felt sad that it was time to say good-bye to their new friends and to the paradise where they had spent an unforgettable week.

"It's just as well we're leaving; I'm eager to see Timothy," Joel said to console himself.

"We leave at about nine tomorrow," Angie instructed, tossing down half a can of beer and inhaling a cigarette.

"You look tired, Angie," Mushaha remarked.

"These last days have been hairy. I had to fly some food supplies across the border. People are desperate there; it's horrible to see hunger right in front of your eyes," she said.

"That tribe comes from a very noble race. They used

to live a dignified life; they fished and hunted and planted a few crops, but colonization and war and disease have reduced them to misery. They live off charity now. If it weren't for those food packages they receive, they'd all be dead by now. Half the people of Africa live below the subsistence level," Michael explained.

"What does that mean?" asked Nadia.

"That they don't have enough to live on."

With that statement the guide put an end to the after-dinner conversation, which had already lasted well past midnight, and announced that it was time to go to the tents. An hour later peace reigned over the camp.

During the night only one guard was assigned to keep watch and feed the bonfires, but soon he, too, drifted off to sleep. As the camp rested, life seethed around them: Beneath the magnificent starry sky roamed hundreds of animal species that came out by night to hunt for food and water. The African night was a true concert of voices: the occasional trumpeting of elephants, hyenas barking in the distance, the screams of mandrills frightened by a leopard, croaking frogs, and the incessant song of the cicadas.

Shortly before dawn Kate suddenly woke with alarm; she thought she had heard some noise very close by. "I must have dreamed it," she murmured, turning over on her cot. She tried to calculate how long she had slept. Her bones creaked, her muscles ached, and her legs were cramping. She felt every one of her sixty-seven hard-lived years; her frame was battered from her adventures. "I'm too old for this kind of life," the writer mused, but almost immediately retracted that thought, convinced that any other life was not worth living. She suffered more lying in bed than from the fatigue of the day. The hours in the tent passed at a paralyzing pace. Then again she heard the sound that had waked her. She couldn't identify it, but it sounded like a scraping or scratching.

The last mists of sleep dissipated completely and Kate sat straight up on her cot, her throat dry and her heart pounding. No doubt about it; something was out there, just on the other side of the cloth tent. Very carefully, trying not to make any noise, she felt in the darkness for her flashlight, which she always kept nearby. When she held it in her hand, she realized she was sweating with fear; her fingers were too moist to switch it on. She kept trying, but was diverted when she heard the voice of Nadia, with whom she shared the tent.

"Shhh, Kate! Don't turn on the light," the girl whispered.

"What is it?"

"Lions. Don't be afraid," Nadia answered.

The flashlight dropped from the writer's hand. She felt her bones turn to mush, and a scream from her gut lodged in her throat. A single slash of a lion's claws would rip the thin nylon tent and the cat would be on them. It wouldn't be the first time that a tourist had died that way on safari. During their treks they had seen lions so close that they could count their teeth; she had decided that she didn't care to meet them in the flesh. An image flashed through her mind: early Christians in the Roman coliseum, condemned to be eaten alive by the beasts. Sweat ran down her face as she groped on the ground for the flashlight, by now entangled in the mosquito netting that hung around her cot. She heard the purring of a great cat and new scratchings.

This time the tent shook, as if a tree had dropped on it. Terrified, Kate dimly realized that Nadia was purring back. Finally she found the flashlight and with wet, trembling fingers she switched it on. She saw Nadia crouching down, her face against the cloth of the tent, enthralled, engaged in an exchange of deep purrs with the beast on the other side. The scream that had been stuck inside Kate escaped as a terrible howl that took Nadia by surprise, literally knocking her off her feet. Kate swept up the girl in one arm and began trying to pull her. New screams, this time accompanied by the chilling roars of the lions, shattered the quiet of the camp.

Within a few seconds, staff and visitors were outside, despite the specific instructions of Mushaha, who had warned them a hundred times of the dangers of leaving their tents at night. Kate was still tugging at Nadia, dragging her outside as the girl kicked and struggled, trying to get free. Half the tent collapsed in the tug of war, and one of the nettings broke lose and fell over them, enveloping them completely. They looked like two larvae trying to break out of a cocoon. Alexander, the first to arrive, ran to them and tried to untangle them from the netting. Once she was free, Nadia pushed him away, furious because her conversation with the lions had been interrupted in such an uncivilized fashion.

As that was going on, Mushaha fired his pistol into the air, and the roars of the lions faded into the distance. The guards lighted torches, sheathed their weapons, and set off to explore the area around the camp. By then the elephants were in an uproar, and their keepers were trying to calm them before they escaped their corrals and stampeded through the camp. Crazed by the smell of the lions, the three pygmy chimps were chattering and clinging to the first person who came by. Borobá had leaped onto Alexander, who was ineffectually trying to pull him off his head by tugging his tail. In all the confusion, no one had any idea what had happened.

Joel had run outside yelling, his heart in his mouth.

"Snakes! A python!"

"Lions," Kate corrected.

Joel stopped short, bewildered.

"It's not snakes?" He hesitated.

"No, only lions," Kate repeated.

"And you woke me up for that?" sputtered the photographer.

"For God's sake, man, cover your privates!" joked Angie, who had appeared in her pajamas.

Only then did Joel realize that he was stark naked; he backed off toward his tent, covering himself with both hands.

Michael Mushaha returned shortly afterward with the news that they had found the tracks of several lions around the compound, and that Kate and Nadia's tent had been ripped.

"This is the first time anything like this has happened in the camp. Those animals have never attacked before," he commented, worried.

"They weren't attacking us!" Nadia interrupted

"Oh. So it was only a courtesy call," said Kate, indignant.

"They came to say hello! If you hadn't started shrieking, Kate, we would still be talking!"

Nadia turned and took refuge in her tent, which she had to crawl into since only two poles were left standing.

"Pay no attention to her, it's just adolescence. It will pass, everyone gets over it," was the opinion of Joel, who had reappeared wrapped in a towel.

The others stood around talking, and no one went back to sleep. They stirred up the fires and left the torches lighted. Borobá and the three pygmy chimps, all four stiff with fright, took cover as far away from Nadia's tent as possible, where they could still smell the scent of the beasts. Shortly after, they heard the winging bats announcing the dawn, then the cooks beginning to brew coffee and fry bacon and eggs for breakfast.

"I've never seen you so nervous. You're getting soft in your old age, Grandmother," said Alexander, handing the first cup of coffee to Kate.

"Do not call me Grandmother, Alexander."

"I won't, if you won't call me Alexander. My name is Jaguar, at least to my family and friends."

"Aggh. Don't be such a pest," she replied, burning her lips with the first sip of the steaming beverage.

CHAPTER THREE

The Missionary

✦

THE SAFARI STAFF LOADED THE equipment into Land
Rovers and then by elephant accompanied the
International Geographic party to where Angie's plane
waited in an open area, two miles from the camp. For
the visitors it was their last ride. The haughty Kobi,
who had carried Nadia all that week, sensed the part-
ing and seemed downcast, as were all the guests.
Borobá, too, was dejected; he was leaving behind the
three chimps that had become good friends; for the
first time in his life, he had to admit that there were
monkeys almost as clever as he was.

As they approached the Cessna Caravan, they could
see the signs of its years of use and the many miles it
had flown. A logo on the side announced its arrogant
name: *Super Hawk*. Angie had painted the head, eyes,
beak, and claws of a bird of prey on the plane, but over
time the paint had flaked and in the shimmering
morning light the vehicle much more closely resembled a pathetic molting hen. The travelers shivered at

the thought that it was their only means of transportation—all except Nadia, because compared to the ancient, rusty little plane her father flew around the Amazon, Angie's *Super Hawk* looked super indeed. The same band of ill-behaved mandrills that had drunk Kate's vodka were squatting on the wings of the metal bird busily grooming each other, picking off lice with great concentration, the way humans often do. In many places in the world, Kate had seen the same loving ritual of delousing that united families and created bonds among friends. Sometimes children got in line, ranging from the smallest to the largest, to inspect one another's heads. She smiled, thinking how in the United States the mere word "lice" evoked shudders of horror. Angie began lobbing rocks and insults at the baboons, to which they responded with Olympian scorn, refusing to budge an inch until the elephants were practically on top of them.

Mushaha handed Angie a vial of animal tranquilizer.

"This is the last one I have. Can you bring me a box on your next trip?" he asked.

"Of course."

"Take this one as a sample; there are several different brands, and you might get the wrong one. This is the one I need."

"No problem," said Angie, putting the vial in the plane's emergency kit for safekeeping.

They had finished stowing the luggage in the plane when a man no one had ever seen before burst out of the nearby undergrowth. He was wearing blue jeans, worn midcalf boots, and a filthy cotton shirt. On his head was a cloth hat, and on his back a knapsack onto which he had tied a clay pot black with soot and a machete. He was a short man, thin and bony and bald. His skin was very pale, his eyebrows dark and bushy, and the lenses of his eyeglasses were thick as bottle glass.

"Good day, ladies and gentlemen," he said in Spanish, and immediately repeated the greeting in English and French.

He introduced himself: "I am Brother Fernando, a Catholic missionary," first shaking Mushaha's hand and then the others'.

"How did you get here?" Mushaha asked.

"With the help of some truck drivers, but most of the way walking."

"On foot? From where? There are no villages for miles around."

"The roads are long, but they all lead to God," the man replied.

He explained that he was Spanish, born in Galicia, although it had been many years since he had visited his homeland. Almost as soon as he left the seminary, he had been sent to Africa, and he had been there for more than thirty years, carrying out his ministry in a number of different countries. His most recent assignment had been a village in Rwanda, where he worked with other missionaries and three nuns in a small compound. It was a region that had been devastated by the cruelest war the continent had witnessed. Refugees swarmed from one end of the country to the other, escaping the violence, but it always caught up with them. The ground was covered with ashes and blood; no crops had been planted for years; people who escaped the bullets and knives fell victim to hunger and illness; starving widows and orphans wandered roads straight out of hell, many of them wounded or mutilated.

"Death is having a ball in those parts," the missionary concluded.

"I've seen it, too," Angie added. "More than a million people have died, the slaughter continues, and the rest of the world doesn't seem to care."

"Here in Africa is where human life started. We all descended from Adam and Eve, whom scientists say were African. This is the earthly paradise mentioned in the Bible. God wanted this to be a garden where his creatures would live in peace and abundance, but you see what hatred and human stupidity have made of it," the missionary added with a preacher's zeal.

"And you were escaping from the war?" Kate asked.

"My fellow workers and I received orders to evacuate the mission after the rebels burned our school, but I am not another refugee. No, the truth is that I have a task to fulfill. I must locate two missionaries who have disappeared."

"In Rwanda?" asked Mushaha.

"No, they are in a village called Ngoubé. Here, look."

Brother Fernando unfolded a map and spread it on the ground to show them the point where his companions had disappeared. Everyone grouped around him.

"This is the most inaccessible, the hottest, and least hospitable area of equatorial Africa. Civilization has not as yet reached here. There is no way to get around other than by canoe on the river, and there are no telephones or radios," the missionary explained.

"Then how is it possible to communicate with the missionaries?" Alexander asked.

"Letters take months, but my brothers were able to send us news from time to time. Life there is hard, and very dangerous. The region is controlled by one Maurice Mbembelé. He is a psychopath, a madman, a brute who has been accused of acts as horrific as cannibalism. We have heard nothing of our brothers for several months. We're very worried."

Alexander studied Brother Fernando's map, which still lay on the ground. That piece of paper could not give even a vague idea of the immensity of the continent, with its multitude of countries and six hundred million people. During that weeklong safari with Michael Mushaha, Alexander had learned a lot, but he nevertheless felt lost before the complexity of Africa, with its diverse climates, geography, cultures, beliefs, races, and languages. The place the missionary's finger was pointing to meant nothing to him; he understood only that Ngoubé was in another country.

"I have to go there," said Brother Fernando.

"How?" Angie asked.

"You must be Angie Ninderera, the owner of this plane, right? I have heard a lot about you. They told me that you can fly anywhere—"

"Hey! Don't even think of asking me to take you there, man!" exclaimed Angie, holding up both hands in a defensive gesture.

"Why not? This is an emergency."

"Because," Angie replied, "where you mean to go is a swampy region covered with trees; there's no place to land. Because no one with an ounce of sense goes any-where near there. Because I have been hired by *International Geographic* magazine to bring these jour-nalists back to the capital safe and sound. Because I have other things to do. And, finally, because I don't, somehow, see you paying me for my trouble."

"God will repay you, I have no doubt," said the mis-sionary.

"Listen, it seems to me that your God already has a lot of unpaid debts."

As they were arguing, Alexander took his grand-mother by the arm and led her aside.

"We have to help this man, Kate," he said.

"What are you thinking, Alex . . . I mean, Jaguar?"

"That we could ask Angie to take us to Ngoubé."

"And who's going to pay for it?" Kate queried.

"The magazine, Kate. Just imagine the cool article you can write if we find the missing missionaries."

"And if we don't?"

"It's still news. Don't you see? You won't get another opportunity like this," her grandson pleaded.

"I'll have to check with Joel," replied Kate, in whose eyes Alex immediately recognized the first glint of awakened curiosity.

It didn't seem like a bad idea to Joel, who couldn't go

back home to London anyway because Timothy was still in the hospital.

"Are there snakes there, Kate?"

"More than anywhere in the world, Joel."

"But there are gorillas, too," Alex said to tempt him. "Maybe you can photograph one up close. It would make a great cover for *International Geographic*."

"Well, in that case, I'll go along," Joel decided.

Angie was finally convinced by the roll of bills Kate thrust in her face and the idea of a very difficult flight, a challenge she could not resist. The pilot snagged the money with one fist, lighted the first cigarette of the day, and gave the order to toss some of the baggage into the cabin while she checked the plane's weight distribution and made sure *Super Hawk* was in top operating form.

"This machine is safe, right?" asked Joel, for whom the worst part of his job was snakes and the second-worst part was flying in small planes.

As her only answer, Angie spat some tobacco shreds at his feet. Alex nudged Joel with his elbow. He shared the photographer's feeling that this conveyance did not seem altogether safe, especially considering that it was piloted by an eccentric woman with a case of beer at her feet, who also kept a lighted cigarette clamped between her teeth only a few feet away from the drums of gasoline carried for refueling.

Twenty minutes later the Cessna was loaded and the passengers were in place. There weren't enough seats for everyone, so Alex and Nadia wiggled into a niche among the bundles in the tail; no one used a seat belt because Angie thought it an unnecessary precaution.

"In case there's an accident, the belts wouldn't do anything but keep the bodies from spilling out of the plane," she said.

She started the motors; the sound evoked the smile it always did—one of immeasurable tenderness. The plane shook like a wet dog, coughed a little, and began to bump along the improvised landing strip. Angie shouted a triumphal Comanche yell as the wheels lifted from the ground and her beloved *Hawk* rose toward the skies.

"May God protect us," the missionary murmured, crossing himself, and Joel followed suit.

The view from the air offered a small sample of the variety and beauty of the African landscape. They left behind the nature preserve where they had spent the past week: vast hot, red dirt plains dotted with trees and wild animals. They passed over parched deserts, forests, mountains, lakes, rivers, and villages separated by great distances. The farther they flew toward the horizon, the farther they stepped back in time.

The noise of the motors was a serious obstacle to conversation, but Alexander and Nadia insisted on talking, shouting above the racket. Brother Fernando replied to their endless questions at the same volume. They were heading toward the forests of an area near the equator, he said. Audacious nineteenth-century explorers, and French and Belgian colonizers in the twentieth century, had penetrated that green hell for a brief time, but the mortality rate was so high—eight of every ten men perished of tropical diseases, crimes, or accidents—that they were forced to retreat. After the country's independence, when the foreign colonials withdrew, successive governments had reached out their tentacles toward the most remote villages. They built roads and sent soldiers, teachers, doctors, and bureaucrats, but the jungle and terrible illnesses thwarted civilization. Missionaries determined to spread Christianity at any price were the only ones who persevered in their aim to put down roots in that infernal region.

"You can count fewer than one inhabitant per square mile, and the population is concentrated around the rivers; all the rest is uninhabited," Brother Fernando explained. "No one goes into the swamps. The natives are convinced that spirits live there, and that there are still dinosaurs."

"Fascinating!" said Alexander.

The missionary's description sounded like the mythological Africa he had visualized when his grandmother announced the trip. He had been disillusioned when they reached Nairobi and he found himself in a modern city with tall buildings and bustling traffic. The nearest thing to a warrior he had seen had been in the tribe of nomads who brought the sick child to Mushaha's camp. Even the safari elephants had seemed too tame to him. When he mentioned that to Nadia, she shrugged her shoulders, unable to understand why he felt cheated with his first impression of Africa. She hadn't expected anything in particular. Alexander concluded that if Africa had been populated by extraterrestrials, Nadia would have accepted them as an everyday occurrence, because she never pictured anything in advance. Maybe now, at the place marked on Brother Fernando's map, he would find the magic land he had imagined.

Other than the passenger's thirst, exhaustion, and airsickness, the flight was uneventful. After several hours Angie began to descend through thin clouds.

She pointed to the endless green land below, where they could identify the sinuous line of a single river. They saw absolutely no sign of human life, but they were too high to see villages, even if there were any.

"This is it, I'm sure of it!" Brother Fernando yelled.

"Just as I warned you, there's no place to land!" Angie yelled back.

"Take the plane down, miss, and God will provide," the missionary assured her.

"Well, he better, because we need to refuel!"

The *Super Hawk* began to descend in sweeping circles. As they got closer to earth, the passengers could see that the river was much wider than they'd thought. Angie explained that they would find villages farther south, but Brother Fernando insisted that they had to head northwest, toward the region where his companions had built the mission. Angie circled a couple of times, still descending.

"We're burning up what little gasoline we have left! I'm heading south," she decided finally.

"There, Angie!" Kate pointed suddenly.

Along one side of the river, as if by enchantment, appeared the clear fringe of a shore.

"That strip is narrow and very short, Angie," Kate warned.

"I only need a little over a couple of hundred yards,

but I don't think we have that much," Angie replied.

She circled again to take measure of the open area and check the best angle for her approach.

"It won't be the first time I've landed in less than two hundred yards. Hang on, guys, we're in for a ride!" she announced with another of her typical war cries.

Until that moment Angie had been totally relaxed in her piloting, with a can of beer between her knees and a cigarette between her fingers. Now her attitude changed. She stubbed out her cigarette in the ashtray fastened to the floor with adhesive tape, settled her corpulence in her seat, gripped the wheel with both hands, and got ready to set her course without ever interrupting the steady stream of curses and Comanche yells and appeals to the good luck that according to her had never failed her—after all, why did she wear a fetish around her neck? Kate chorused Angie, yelling till she was hoarse, because she couldn't think of any other way to calm her nerves. Nadia closed her eyes and thought of her father. Alexander opened his eyes wide, invoking his friend, the lama Tensing, whose prodigious mental powers would have been a great boon to them at this moment, but Tensing was far, far away. Brother Fernando started praying aloud in Spanish, and Joel immediately chimed in. At the end of the short strip of open shore, as forbidding as the

Great Wall of China, rose the impenetrable growth of the jungle. They had only one chance to land; if that failed, there wouldn't be enough strip left to allow them to pull up: They would crash into the trees.

Angie lined up *Super Hawk*'s nose and dropped abruptly. The first tree branches scraped the plane's belly. The minute she found herself above the impromptu landing field, Angie felt for the ground, praying it was firm and not strewn with rocks. The plane hit the ground skipping and lurching like a great wounded bird, while chaos was unleashed inside: Bundles flew from one side to another, the passengers banged against the roof, beer cans rolled, and gasoline drums danced. Angie, her hands clamped on the controls, hit the brakes with all her strength, trying to stabilize the plane and not tear off its wings. The engine roared a desperate death rattle, and a strong odor of burned rubber filled the cabin. The machine shook from the struggle to stop and covered the remaining distance in a cloud of sand and smoke.

"The trees!" screamed Kate when they were almost upon them.

Angie did not respond to her client's superfluous observation; she was having no difficulty seeing them. She felt the blend of absolute terror and fascination that coursed through her when her life was on the line:

a sudden discharge of adrenaline that made her skin prickle and her heart race. That joyful terror was what she loved most about her job. Her muscles locked in the brutal effort to dominate the plane; she was taking on metal and motor personally, like a cowboy riding a wild bull. Suddenly, when the trees were six feet away and the passengers all thought their moment had come, *Super Hawk* tilted forward, gave one last tremendous shudder, and buried its nose in the sand.

"Damnation!" yelled Angie.

"Curb your tongue, woman," said Brother Fernando in a wavering voice from the back of the cabin, where his weakly kicking legs were all that could be seen from beneath piles of photographic equipment. "Don't you see that God provided us a place to land?"

"Well, tell him to send me a mechanic as well, because we have problems," Angie bellowed back.

"Let's not get hysterical," Kate ordered. "First of all we need to examine the damage." She prepared to jump out as the others crawled and pulled themselves toward the door. The first one outside was poor Borobá, who seldom had been so frightened in all his life. Alexander saw that Nadia's face was covered with blood.

"Eagle!" he cried, trying to dig her out from bundles, cameras, and seats that had wrenched free of the floor.

When at last everyone was outside and they could

evaluate the situation, it turned out that no one was injured; Nadia had no more than a nosebleed. The plane, on the other hand, was damaged indeed.

"Just what I was afraid of. The propeller's bent," said Angie.

"Is that serious?" asked Alexander.

"Under normal circumstances it wouldn't be. If I can get another propeller, I can change it myself, but way out here, we're in the soup. Where am I going to get a replacement?"

Before Brother Fernando could open his mouth, Angie confronted him, hands on her hips.

"And if you don't want to see me *really* mad, don't tell me that your God will provide!"

Prudently, the missionary held his tongue.

"Where are we exactly?" asked Kate.

"I don't have the faintest idea," Angie admitted.

Brother Fernando consulted his map and told them that he felt sure they were not far from Ngoubé, the village where his companions had established the mission.

"We're surrounded with tropical jungle and swamps. There's no way out of here without a boat," said Angie.

"Then let's build a fire. A cup of tea and a sip or two of vodka won't hurt at all," Kate proposed.

CHAPTER FOUR

Incommunicado in the Jungle

As NIGHT FELL, THE journeyers decided to make camp near the trees, where they would be better protected.

"Are there pythons in this part of the world?" asked Joel, thinking of the near fatal embrace of an anaconda in the Amazon.

"Pythons aren't a problem because you can see them coming and shoot them. Much worse are the Gabon viper and forest cobra. Their poison kills in a matter of minutes," said Angie.

"Did we bring an antidote?"

"There is no antidote for those bites. I'm more worried about crocodiles; those monsters eat everything," commented Angie.

"But they stay in the river, don't they?" asked Alexander.

"They're also ferocious on land. When animals come down to drink at night, crocs snatch them and drag them to the bottom of the river. Not a pleasant death," Angie detailed.

She always carried a revolver and a rifle in her plane, though she had never had to fire them. In view of the fact that they would have to take turns standing guard through the night, she demonstrated to the others how to use them. They took a few shots and found that the weapons were in good condition, but none of them was able to hit a target only a few yards away. Brother Fernando refused to even try, because, according to him, firearms are tools of the devil. His experience in the war in Rwanda had left him badly scarred.

"This is my protection, this scapulary," he said, showing them a piece of cloth he wore on a cord around his neck.

"This what?" asked Kate, who never had heard the word before.

"It's a holy object, blessed by the pope," said Joel, showing them a similar one he wore.

For Kate, who had been brought up in the sobriety of a Protestant church, the Catholic faith was as picturesque as African religious ceremonies.

"I have an amulet, too, but I don't think it will save me from ending up in the jaws of a crocodile someday," Angie said, showing them a small leather pouch.

"Don't compare that witchcraft fetish to a scapulary!" protested Brother Fernando, offended.

"What's the difference?" asked Alexander, who was very interested.

"One represents the power of Christ, and the other is pagan superstition."

"Our beliefs are religion; everybody else's are superstition," commented Kate.

She had often repeated that sentence to her grandson, hoping to pound respect for different cultures into his head. Other favorite sayings of hers were, "We speak a *language*, anything else is a *dialect*," and "White people create *art*; other races make *crafts*." Alexander had tried to explain his grandmother's statements in his social science class, but no one had understood the irony.

A passionate discussion about Christian faith and African animism ensued, in which everyone in the group participated except Alexander, who was wearing an amulet of his own around his neck and thought it best to keep silent, and Nadia, who was walking up and down the open shoreline from one end to the other, deeply engrossed and accompanied by Borobá. Alexander went to join them.

"What are you looking for, Eagle?" he asked.

Nadia bent down and picked up some bits of rope from the sand.

"I found several of these," she said.

"It must be some kind of vine."

"No. I think they're something someone has made."

"What can they be?"

"I don't know, but it means that someone was here not too long ago, and maybe he will be back. We're not as isolated as Angie believes," Nadia deduced.

"I hope they aren't cannibals."

"Yes, that would really be bad luck," she said, thinking of what she'd heard the missionary say about the madman who ruled the region.

"I don't see human footprints anywhere," Alexander commented.

"Or animals', either. The earth is soft, and the rain has washed everything away."

Several times a day, there was a downpour that drenched them as effectively as standing in a shower, then ended as suddenly as it had begun. Those cloudbursts kept them wringing wet, yet didn't offer any relief from the heat; just the opposite, the humidity made things even more unbearable. The stranded travelers set up Angie's tent, into which five of them could crowd as the sixth stood guard. At Brother Fernando's suggestion, they looked for animal droppings to make a fire; it was the only way to keep the mosquitoes at bay and at the same time mask their scent, which might attract wild animals. The missionary warned them against bugs that lay their eggs under fingernails and toenails; those pockets become infected, making it necessary to pry up the nails with a knife and scrape out the larvae, a procedure akin to Chinese torture. To prevent that, they rubbed their hands and feet with gasoline. He also warned them not to leave any food in the open because the ants it attracted could be more dangerous than crocodiles. An invasion of termites was a terrifying sight; in their passing they wiped out every living thing, leaving nothing behind but bare earth. Alexander and Nadia had heard about those insects in the Amazon, but now they learned that the African species were even more voracious. As dusk fell they were set upon by a swarm of tiny bees, the insufferable *mopani*; despite the smoke, the pests invaded the camp and swarmed over every inch of their skin, even their eyelids.

"They don't bite; they just drink your sweat. It's better not to try to shoo them off," the missionary told them. "You'll get used to them."

"Look there!" called Joel.

An ancient turtle with a shell more than three feet across was creeping along the shore at the water's edge.

"He's probably more than a hundred years old," Brother Fernando calculated.

"I make a delicious turtle soup!" exclaimed Angie, picking up a machete. "You have to swing the minute they stick their head out—"

"Don't even think of killing it," interrupted Alexander.

"That shell's worth a lot of money," said Angie.

"We can eat tinned sardines for supper," Nadia reminded her. She, too, was opposed to the idea of eating the defenseless turtle.

"It's not a good idea to kill it. It has a strong odor, and that will attract dangerous predators," added Brother Fernando.

The centenarian ambled on along the riverbank at its calm pace, never suspecting how near it had come to ending its days in a pot.

The sun went down, the shadows of the nearby trees lengthened, and finally it was cool.

"Don't look over this way, Brother Fernando, because I'm going to take a dip and I don't want to entice you." Angie laughed.

"I would advise you, miss, not to go near the river. You never know what you might find in the water," the missionary replied dryly, not looking at her.

But Angie had already taken off her slacks and blouse and was running toward the riverbank in her underwear. She had sense enough not to go into water any deeper than to her knees, and she was watchful, ready to fly out of the river in case of danger. With the same tin cup she used to drink her coffee, she began emptying water over her head with obvious pleasure. The others followed her example, except for Borobá, who hated getting wet, and the missionary, who stood with his back to the river, concentrating on preparing a meager meal of beans and tinned sardines.

Nadia was the first to see the hippopotamuses. In the shadows of dusk, they blended into the dark water, so the group became aware of their presence only when they were very near. There were two adults—smaller than those on Michael Mushaha's preserve—enjoying the water a few feet away from where they were bathing. The third animal, their offspring, they saw only later, peering from between the monumental rear ends of its parents. Quietly, doing nothing to provoke them, the friends stepped out of the water and returned to camp. The huge animals showed no curiosity at all toward the humans; they continued to bathe calmly for a long while, until it was so dark that they disappeared in the blackness. Their deeply creased skin was thick and gray like that of the elephants. Their ears were small and round, and their mahogany eyes very bright. Two pouches swung from their upper jaws, cushioning the enormous, square canines that were capable of biting through an iron pipe.

"They take a mate, and they are more faithful than most humans," explained Brother Fernando. "They have one calf at a time and look after it for years."

After the sun went down, night had fallen very quickly and the group was surrounded by the impenetrable darkness of the forest. Only in the small clearing on the shore where they had crash-landed could the moon be seen in the sky. The solitude was absolute. They set up a schedule to sleep in shifts while one of them stood guard and fed the fire. Nadia, who had been excused from responsibility because of her age, insisted on sitting up with Alexander during his turn. Many of the animals that came during the night to drink at the river were confused by the smoke, the fire, and the scent of human beings. The most timid retreated, frightened, but others sniffed the air, hesitated, and finally, prodded by thirst, approached. The instructions of Brother Fernando, who had studied the flora and fauna of Africa for thirty years, were not to disturb them. Usually they did not attack humans, he said, unless they were hungry or provoked.

"That's in theory. In practice they're unpredictable and might attack at any moment," Angie refuted.

"The fire will keep them some distance away. I think we're safe here on the shore. It will be more dangerous in the forest," said Brother Fernando.

Angie cut him off. "Yes, but we don't plan to go into the forest."

"Are you thinking of staying here forever?" the missionary asked.

"We can't get out of here by land. The only possibility is the river."

"Swimming?" Brother Fernando persisted.

"We could build a raft," Alexander suggested.

"You've read too many adventure novels, young man," the missionary replied.

"We'll decide that tomorrow; right now, let's rest," Kate ordered.

Alexander and Nadia's shift began at three in the morning. With Borobá they would watch the sun come up. Sitting back to back, weapons on their knees, they talked in whispers. They always stayed in contact when they were separated, but even so they had a thousand things to tell each other when they met. Their friendship was profound, and they were sure that it would last throughout their lifetimes. True friendship, they believed, survives the passing of time, is selfless and generous, and asks nothing in return except loyalty. They had never actually discussed it, but both protected their affection from the curiosity of others. They loved each other without making a great show of it, discreetly and quietly. They shared dreams, thoughts, emotions, and secrets by e-mail. They knew each other so well that sometimes words weren't necessary to express what they were thinking.

More than once Alexander's mother had asked him if Nadia was "his girl," and he always denied it more emphatically than was necessary. She wasn't "his girl" in the common sense of the term. The mere question offended him. His relationship with Nadia could not be compared to the fits of love that struck his friends or to his own fantasies about Cecilia Burns, the girl he had thought he would marry ever since he started school. The feelings between Nadia and him were unique, untouchable, precious. He realized that such an intense and pure relationship was not common among teens, and that is why he didn't talk about her. No one would understand.

. . .

An hour later the stars began to disappear, one by one, and day began to dawn: first a soft glow in the sky that soon became a spectacular blaze flooding the landscape with orange reflections. A variety of birds filled the sky, and a concert of birdsong waked the rest of the party. They immediately sprang into action, some stirring the fire and preparing something to eat, others helping Angie remove the propeller with the hope that it could be repaired.

They had to pick up sticks to stave off the monkeys that descended on the small camp to steal food. The battle left them exhausted. The monkeys withdrew some distance down the beach and watched from there, awaiting a moment's inattention to attack again.

The heat and humidity were crushing: Everyone's clothing stuck to their bodies, their hair was wet, their skin burning. The forest exuded a strong odor of decomposing organic matter that blended with the stench of the excrement they had used for their fire. They were besieged with thirst, but they had to conserve the last reserves of bottled water they had in the plane. Brother Fernando suggested using water from the river, but Kate said that it would give them typhus or cholera.

"We can boil it, but with this heat there's no way to

cool it down; we'd have to drink it hot," Angie added.

"Then let's have tea," Kate concluded.

The missionary used the jug hanging from his pack to bring water from the river and also to boil it. The water was the color of iron oxide, metallic in taste, and had a strange sweetish, almost nauseating smell.

Borobá was the only one of them to venture into the forest; everyone else was afraid of getting lost in the thick undergrowth. Nadia noticed that he kept darting back and forth, with a look that at first seemed to be of curiosity but soon resembled desperation. She called Alexander, and they went after the monkey.

"Don't go far, children," Kate warned.

"We'll be right back," her grandson replied.

Without a moment's hesitation, Borobá led them through the trees. As he jumped lightly from branch to branch, Nadia and Alexander fought their way forward, beating a path through thick ferns and praying they wouldn't step on a snake or come face-to-face with a leopard.

Alexander and Nadia plunged through the vegetation, never losing sight of Borobá. It seemed to them that they were following a faint path through the forest, maybe a very old trail that had filled in with plants but was still used by animals going to the river to drink. The pair was covered with bugs from head to foot; faced with the impossibility of getting rid of the pests, they had no choice but to resign themselves to them. They tried not to think of the number of illnesses transmitted by insects, from malaria to the lethal sleep induced by the tsetse fly, whose victims sank into a deep lethargy in which they languished until they died, trapped in the labyrinth of their nightmares. In places, they had to sweep aside enormous spiderwebs before they could continue, and from time to time they sank up to their calves in gluey mud.

Suddenly through the unrelenting sounds of the forest they could hear something similar to a human lament, shocking enough to make them stop and listen. Borobá began jumping up and down nervously, indicating that they needed to keep going. Some yards farther on, they saw what was disturbing him. Alexander, who was in the lead, came within a few feet of falling into a pit yawning at his feet, a kind of deep trench. The cry was originating from a dark form that at first sight they took to be a large dog.

"What is it?" murmured Alexander, stepping back and not daring to raise his voice.

Borobá's screeches grew louder; the creature in the

hole moved, and then they could see it was some kind of simian. It was tangled in a net that had completely immobilized it. The animal looked up and when it saw them began to roar and bare its teeth.

"It's a gorilla," said Nadia. "It can't get out."

"It looks like it's in a trap."

"We have to get it out," Nadia said.

"How? It might bite us. . . ."

Nadia leaned down toward the trapped animal and began to talk to it as she did with Borobá.

"What is it saying?" Alexander asked her.

"I don't know whether it understands me. Not all apes speak the same language, Jaguar. On the safari I could communicate with the chimpanzees, but not the mandrills."

"Those mandrills were scoundrels, Eagle. They wouldn't have listened to you even if they did understand you."

"I don't know the language of these gorillas, but I suppose it must be something like that of other apes."

"Tell it to stay quiet, and we'll see if we can free it from the net."

Little by little, Nadia's voice calmed the imprisoned animal, but when they tried to come closer, it bared its teeth again and growled.

"It has a baby!" Alexander cried.

The gorilla's offspring was tiny—it couldn't have been more than a few weeks old—and it was clinging desperately to its mother's shaggy coat.

"We need to go get help. We're going to have to cut the net," Nadia decided.

They hurried back to the river as quickly as the terrain allowed and told the rest of the party what they had found.

"That animal could attack us," Brother Fernando warned. "Gorillas are peaceful, but females with young are always dangerous."

Nadia, however, had already laid her hands on a knife and started back, so everyone followed her. Joel could scarcely believe his good fortune: He was going to photograph a gorilla after all. Brother Fernando armed himself with his machete and a long stick. Angie carried the revolver and the rifle. Borobá led them straight to the trap, but when the gorilla saw herself surrounded by human faces she became frantic.

"This is a time when Mushaha's tranquilizer gun would come in very handy," Angie observed.

"She's terribly afraid. I'll try to get near her; you wait back there," Nadia directed.

Everyone stepped back several feet and crouched down among the ferns as Nadia and Alexander moved forward inch by inch, pausing, waiting, creeping a little closer. Nadia kept up a constant, soothing monologue, which seemed to calm the poor trapped animal, because after several minutes, the grunting stopped.

"Jaguar, look up there," Nadia whispered into her friend's ear.

Alexander looked up and high in the treetop saw a black, shiny face with close-set eyes and flattened nose observing them attentively.

"It's another gorilla. And it's much bigger than this one!" Alexander replied, also in a murmur.

"Don't look it in the eye. That's a threat to them; it might get angry," she counseled.

The other members of the group also saw the great ape, but no one moved. Joel's hands were tickling to focus his camera, but Kate dissuaded him with a sharp glance. The opportunity to be at such close proximity to these large creatures was so rare that they couldn't ruin it with a false move. A half hour passed and nothing happened; the gorilla in the tree did not move from its observation post, and the figure entangled in the net below was silent. Only her agitated breathing and the way she was holding her baby close betrayed her anguish.

Nadia began to crawl toward the trap, watched by the terrified female from the pit and by the male overhead. Alexander followed with the knife in his teeth, feeling vaguely ridiculous, as if he were in some Tarzan movie. When Nadia reached out to touch the netted animal, the tree branches where the larger gorilla sat swayed ominously.

"If he attacks my grandson, kill him right where he sits," Kate breathed to Angie.

Angie didn't respond. She was afraid that even if the animal were only three feet away she wouldn't be able to shoot it: The rifle was trembling in her hands.

The female never took her eyes off Nadia and Alexander as they crawled toward her, but she seemed a little more calm, as if she had understood the reassurances that Nadia repeated over and over that those humans were not the same ones who had set the trap.

"Easy, easy, we're going to get you out," Nadia kept murmuring, like a litany.

Finally the girl's hand touched the black pelt of the gorilla, which shrank away from the contact and showed her teeth. Nadia, however, did not remove her hand, and gradually the animal relaxed. At a sign from Nadia, Alexander began cautiously to drag himself toward her on his elbows. Very slowly, so as not to startle the frightened creature, he, too, began to stroke the gorilla's back, until she was comfortable with his presence. He filled his lungs with a deep breath, rubbed the amulet on his chest to give himself courage, and gripped the knife to cut some of the rope. The animal's reaction when she felt the metal blade so close to her hide was to draw up into a ball, protecting the baby with her body. Nadia's voice came from somewhere far away, penetrating her terrified mind, calming her; at her back she felt the friction of the knife and the tugging at the net. Cutting the rope turned out to take longer than expected, but finally Alexander succeeded in opening a hole large enough to free the prisoner. He signaled Nadia, and they both scooted back a few feet.

"Out! You can get out now!" she ordered.

Brother Fernando squirmed close to Alexander and handed him his stick, which the youth used to delicately prod the huddled form beneath the net. That had the desired effect. The gorilla raised her head, sniffed the air, and looked around her with curiosity. It took her some minutes to comprehend that she could move, and then she stood up and shook free of the net. When Alexander and Nadia saw her standing up with her baby at her breast, they had to cover their mouths to keep from yelling with excitement. They didn't move a hair. The gorilla crouched down, clutching her baby to her chest with one hand, and sat staring at the two young people with deep concentration.

Alexander shivered when it dawned on him how close the animal was. He felt the warmth of her body, and a black, wrinkled face swam only three or four inches from his own. He closed his eyes, sweating. When he opened them again, he saw a blurred, rosy muzzle filled with yellow teeth. His glasses were fogged over, but he didn't take them off. The gorilla's breath struck him square in the nose; it had the agreeable scent of freshly mowed grass. Suddenly the curious hand of the baby gripped a lock of his hair and tugged. Alexander, choking with happiness, stretched out one finger and the baby gorilla grabbed it as a human child would. The mother was not pleased with that show of confidence, however, and she gave Alexander a shove that knocked him flat, though she wasn't being aggressive. She uttered one emphatic grunt, in the tone of someone asking a question, and with two leaps bounded off to the tree in which the male was watching, and all three faded into the foliage. Nadia helped her friend to his feet.

"Did you see that? It touched me," yelled Alexander, hopping with excitement.

"Well done," Brother Fernando said approvingly.

"Who could have set out that net?" asked Nadia, thinking that it must be of the same fiber as the bits of rope she had found by the river.

CHAPTER FIVE

The Bewitched Forest

✦

BACK IN CAMP, WHILE THE others discussed the recent adventure, Joel improvised a fishing pole from a length of cane, some string, and bent wire, and sat on the riverbank hoping to catch something to eat. Brother Fernando agreed with Nadia's theory that there was hope that someone would come to help them, because the net indicated a human presence. At some moment the hunters would return to check the pit.

"Why would they be hunting gorillas?" Alexander wanted to know. "The meat's terrible, and the skin is ugly."

"The meat is edible if there's no other choice. The organs are used in witchcraft; they make masks from the hide and skulls, and they sell the hands for ashtrays. Tourists love them," the missionary explained.

"That's horrible!"

"In the mission in Rwanda, we had a two-year-old gorilla, the only one we were able to save. They killed the mothers and sometimes brought the abandoned babies to us. They're a sensitive breed and often die of melancholy . . . if they don't die of hunger first."

"By the way, isn't anybody hungry?" asked Alexander.

"It was dumb to let that turtle go; we could have dined in style," Angie noted.

The persons responsible for the centenarian's reprieve said nothing. Angie was right: In such circumstances they couldn't allow themselves the luxury of sentimentality; survival came first.

"How is it going with the radio in the plane?" asked Kate.

"I've sent out several SOS calls, but I don't think anyone received them. We're a long way from nowhere. I'll keep trying to contact Mushaha. I promised him we'd call in twice a day. Surely he'll be surprised not to hear from us," Angie replied.

"At any moment someone will miss us and come looking for us," Kate consoled them.

"I think we've had it," blubbered Angie. "My plane is in pieces, we're lost, and we're hungry."

"What a pessimist you are, woman! God may put a rope around your neck, but he doesn't pull it tight. You'll see, everything we need will be provided," Brother Fernando replied.

Angie seized the missionary's arms and hoisted him a few inches off the ground, until they were eye to eye.

"If you had listened to me, we wouldn't be in this pickle!" she spit out, shooting sparks.

Kate intervened. "It was my decision to come here, Angie."

The group scattered across the beach, each occupied in his own project. With the help of Alexander and Nadia, Angie had managed to remove the propeller. After carefully examining it, she confirmed what she had suspected: They would not be able to repair it with the tools at hand. They were trapped.

Joel hadn't really believed that anything would strike at his primitive fishhook, so he nearly fell backward with surprise when he felt a tug on the line. Everyone came running to help him, and finally, after a long struggle, they hauled a good-sized carp from the water. The fish thrashed on the sand for some minutes, which was acute torture for Nadia, who couldn't bear to see animals suffer.

"It's the way of nature, child. Some die so others can live," Brother Fernando consoled her.

He didn't add that God had sent them the carp, which was what he truly believed, because he didn't want to provoke Angie's wrath anew. They cleaned the fish, wrapped it in leaves, and roasted it: Nothing had ever tasted so delicious. By then the clearing was blazing like an inferno. They improvised some shade, rigging canvas on long poles, and lay down to rest, observed by the monkeys and the large green lizards that had come out to soak in the sun.

They were all drowsing, sweating beneath the insufficient shade of the canvas, when a veritable whirlwind blew in from the forest at the far end of the beach, raising clouds of sand. The furor of its arrival was so stupefying that at first they all thought it must be a rhinoceros. At closer view, however, they saw it was a huge boar, with bristly hair and menacing tusks. The beast was blindly charging the camp, giving them no time to grab the weapons they had laid aside during siesta. They barely had time to scramble away before it reached them, crashing against the poles that held up the canvas and sending everything to the ground. From the ruins of the tent, it observed them with malevolent eyes, huffing and snorting.

As Angie ran to find her revolver, her movement caught the attention of the animal, which readied a new attack. Its front hooves raked the sand; it lowered its head and headed straight for Angie, whose considerable flesh presented a perfect target.

Just as Angie's fate seemed inevitable, Brother Fernando stepped between her and the boar, waggling a piece of canvas. The beast stopped short, swerved, and threw itself at the missionary, but at the instant of contact he sidestepped gracefully. The boar lunged past, furious, and charged anew, but once again its only victim was the canvas; it didn't even graze its true target. In the interim Angie had retrieved her revolver, but she didn't dare shoot because the animal was circling around Brother Fernando, so close that the two were a single swirl of movement.

The travelers realized that they were witnessing the most original "bull" fight ever. The missionary was flourishing the canvas as he would a scarlet cape, provoking the beast and goading it with shouts of *"Olé!"* and *"Toro! Toro!"* He was bamboozling it, he was dancing before it, he was maddening it. In a short time, he had exhausted the boar; it was drooling, near collapse, its legs trembling. At that point Brother Fernando turned his back and, with the supreme arrogance of a torero, walked a few steps away, dragging his cape, as the boar tottered on its feet. Angie seized the instant to kill it with two shots to the head. A loud chorus of applause and cheers greeted Brother Fernando's daring feat.

"What good fun that was! It's been thirty-five years since I had a chance to do that," he exclaimed.

He smiled for the first time since they had met him, and he told them that his childhood dream had been to follow in the footsteps of his father, a famous torero, but God had had other plans for him. He had fallen victim to a terrible fever that left him nearly blind, so he couldn't pursue that career. He was wondering what he was going to do with his life when he learned through the parish priest in his village that the church was recruiting missionaries to serve in Africa. He had answered the call only out of the despair of not being able to be a toreador, but soon he discovered he had found his vocation. Being a missionary required the same talents as bullfighting: courage, endurance, and the faith to confront difficulties.

"Fighting bulls is easy. Serving Christ is a little more complex," Brother Fernando concluded.

"To judge by the demonstration you gave us, apparently good eyesight isn't a requirement for either," Angie said warmly—he had saved her life.

"We'll have enough meat for several days, but we need to cook it so it will last a little longer," said Brother Fernando.

"Did you get photographs of the *corrida*?" Kate asked Joel.

The poor fellow had to admit that in the excitement of the moment he had completely forgotten his obligation.

"I have pictures!" shouted Alexander, waving the tiny camera he always had with him.

The only person who knew how to skin and gut the wild boar turned out to be Brother Fernando; he'd seen hogs slaughtered many times in his village. He took off his shirt and got down to work. He didn't have the right knives, so the task was slow and grubby. As he worked, Alexander and Joel, armed with long sticks, beat off the buzzards circling just above their heads. After an hour the edible meat was dressed. They threw the rest into the river, in order not to attract the flies and carnivores that would be drawn by the scent of blood. The missionary dug out the wild pig's tusks and after cleaning them with sand gave them to Alexander and Nadia.

"These are for you to take back to the States as a souvenir," he said.

"That's if we get out of here alive," Angie added.

Brief but heavy rain showers fell through most of the night, making it difficult to keep the fire going. They set a canvas over it, but it kept going out, and finally they resigned themselves to letting it die. The only incident occurred during Angie's shift, something she later described as "a miraculous escape." A crocodile frustrated at not catching its prey at the riverbank was brazen enough to approach the faint glow of the coals and the oil lamp. Angie, crouching beneath a piece of plastic to keep dry, didn't hear it. She became aware of its presence only when it was so close that she could see the gaping jaws less than three feet from her legs. In that split second, the prophecy of Má Bangesé, the marketplace diviner, flashed through her mind. She thought her time had come, yet didn't have the presence of mind to use the rifle by her side. Instinct and fright took over; she sprang up and leaped aside, letting out a series of screams that roused her friends. The crocodile hesitated only a few seconds and lunged forward again. Angie started running, tripped, and fell, rolling to one side to avoid the croc.

The first to answer Angie's screams was Alexander, who had just crawled out of his sleeping bag to report for his shift. Without stopping to think what he was doing, he grabbed the first thing that came to hand and slammed it down as hard as he could on the beast's snout. He screamed louder than Angie and blindly kicked and struck at the animal, half the time missing it completely. By then everyone had run out to help, and Angie, recovered from her surprise, began firing

her weapon. Even without careful aim, one or two bullets hit the target but failed to penetrate the saurian's
thick hide. Finally all the racket, and Alexander's
blows, changed the crocodile's mind about dinner, and
it headed back toward the river, tail slashing indig-
nantly.

"Th—that was a crocodile!" exclaimed Alexander,
stuttering and trembling, unable to believe that he had
battled such a monster.

"Come here, kid, let me give you a kiss; you saved
my life," Angie called, crushing Alex to her ample
bosom.

Alexander felt his ribs creak and was choked by a
scent of fear and gardenia perfume as Angie covered
him with loud smacks, laughing and crying at once.

Joel came over to examine the weapon Alexander
had used.

"That's my camera!" he yipped.

It was. The black leather case was destroyed, but the
heavy German mechanism had withstood the brutal
encounter with the crocodile without apparent
damage.

"I'm really sorry, Joel. The next time I'll use my
own," said Alexander, pulling out his small pocket
camera.

• • •

It stopped raining during the morning, and the entire crew seized the opportunity to wash their clothes with the strong lye soap Angie had in her luggage and lay them out to dry in the sun. They had a breakfast of roast meat, crackers, and tea, and were working on the plan Alexander had suggested the first day—to build a raft and float down river to the nearest village—when two canoes came into view. Their relief and joy were so explosive that they ran toward them howling with jubilation, like the castaways they were. At that reception the canoes slowed, turned, and started moving in the opposite direction. There were two men in each canoe, dressed in shorts and T-shirts. Angie hailed them in English and in all the local languages she could remember, pleading with them to come back, stating that they would gladly pay them for help. The men talked among themselves and finally curiosity, or greed, got the upper hand, and they began cautiously to paddle toward shore. They had established that the group consisted of one robust woman, an odd-looking old woman, two teenagers, a skinny man with thick eyeglasses, and another from whom they could see they had nothing to fear. It was, on the whole, quite a ridiculous group. Once they were convinced that the six strangers presented no danger, despite the weapon in the hands of one of the women, the men waved and got out of the canoes.

The new arrivals introduced themselves as fishermen from a village some miles to the south. They were strong, heavy-bodied—almost square—with very dark skin, and they were armed with machetes. According to Brother Fernando, they belonged to the Bantu peoples.

Because of colonization, the second language of the region was French. To her grandson's surprise, it turned out that Kate spoke passable French and so was able to exchange a few words with the fishermen. Brother Fernando and Angie knew several African languages, and they took a try at anything that could not be communicated in French. They explained their accident to the men, showed them the damaged plane, and asked for their help in getting out of there. The Bantus drank the warm beers they were offered and devoured some strips of boar, but they did not seem interested until a price was reached and Angie handed out cigarettes, which had the effect of softening them up.

In the meantime Alexander had a good look at the canoes, and, as he saw no fishing gear, concluded that the men were lying and could not be trusted. No one among the stranded travelers was easy in his mind.

. . .

While the men in the canoes ate, drank, and smoked, the *International Geographic* party moved away to discuss their situation. Angie's advice was for everyone to stay on guard, for they could be murdered and their goods stolen, though Brother Fernando was sure the men had been sent by heaven to help him accomplish his mission.

"These men will take us upriver toward Ngoubé. According to the map—" he began.

"Are you out of your mind?" Angie interrupted. "We'll head south, to these men's village. There must be some form of communication there. I have to get another propeller and get back to my plane."

"We're very close to Ngoubé. I can't abandon my companions," Brother Fernando rebutted. "Who knows what they're going through."

"Don't you think we already have enough problems?" was the pilot's reply.

"You have no respect for the work of missionaries!"

"And do you respect the African religions? Why do you try to impose your beliefs on us?"

"Be calm, both of you! We have more urgent matters at hand," Kate directed.

"I suggest we split up," Brother Fernando proposed.

"Those who want can go south with you, and those who want to go with me can come to Ngoubé in the second canoe."

"No way! We're much safer together," Kate interrupted.

"Why don't we put it to a vote?" Alexander suggested.

"Because, my boy, in this case democracy doesn't apply," said the missionary dictatorially.

"Then we should allow God to decide," said Alexander.

"How?"

"We'll flip a coin: Heads, we go south; tails, it's to the north. We'll leave it in the hands of God, or of fate, whichever you prefer," the youth outlined, taking a coin from his pocket.

Angie and Brother Fernando hesitated a moment and then both burst out laughing. The idea seemed irresistibly humorous.

"Deal!" they exclaimed in chorus.

Everyone else agreed as well. Alexander handed the coin to Nadia, who tossed it up in the air. They held their breath and watched it fall onto the sand.

"Tails! We're going north!" Brother Fernando shouted in triumph.

"I will give you three days total. If you haven't found your friends in that length of time, we come back. Understood?" roared Angie.

"Five days."

"Four."

"All right, four days and not a minute less."

Convincing the supposed fishermen to take them to the place they pointed out on the map turned out to be more of a job than they had foreseen. The men explained that no one ventured into that area without the authorization of King Kosongo, who had no great love for foreigners.

"King? There are no kings in this country. There is a president and a parliament; it's supposed to be a democracy," said Kate.

Angie clarified that in addition to the national government, certain African clans and tribes had kings, and even queens, whose role was more symbolic than political, just like that of certain sovereigns in Europe.

"Our missionaries mentioned a King Kosongo in their letters, but they had more to say about a Commandant Maurice Mbembelé. It seems that it's the military that's in control," said Brother Fernando.

"Maybe it's not the same village," Angie suggested.

"I have no doubt at all that it's the same."

"I don't think it's a very good idea to walk straight into the jaws of the wolf," Angie commented.

"But we do have to find out what happened to the missionaries," said Kate.

"What do you know about Kosongo, Brother Fernando?" asked Alexander.

"Not much. It seems that Kosongo is a usurper; he was put on the throne by Commandant Mbembelé. There was a queen earlier, but she disappeared. It's supposed that she was murdered; no one has seen her in several years."

"And what did the missionaries say about Mbembelé?" Alexander insisted.

"He studied a couple of years in France but was expelled because of problems with the police," Brother Fernando explained.

He added that once Maurice Mbembelé was back in his country, he joined the army, but he also encountered problems there because of his undisciplined and violent temperament. He was accused of putting down an uprising by burning houses and murdering a number of students. His superiors covered up for him to keep it out of the newspapers, then rid themselves of their problem by sending him to the least known point on the map. They hoped that swamp fevers and mosquito bites would cure him of his bad character—or finish him off once and for all. Mbembelé faded away into the jungle, along with a handful of his most loyal men, and shortly after reappeared in Ngoubé. According to what the missionaries wrote in their letters, Mbembelé set up headquarters in that village and controlled the region from there. He was a tyrant and dealt out the cruelest punishments imaginable. They said that on more than one occasion, he had eaten the liver or heart of his victims.

"That is ritual cannibalism; it's believed that in that way you acquire the courage and strength of your defeated enemy," Kate amplified.

"Idi Amin, a dictator in Uganda, used to serve his ministers for dinner," Angie commented. "Roasted."

"Cannibalism isn't as rare as we believe; I saw it several years ago in Borneo," Kate added.

"Did you really witness acts of cannibalism, Kate?" Alexander asked.

"It happened when I was in Borneo on assignment. I didn't see them actually cooking anyone, if that's what you mean, Alex, but I was told about it firsthand. As a precaution, all I ate was canned beans," his grandmother answered.

"I think I'm going to become a vegetarian," Alexander concluded, nauseated.

Brother Fernando told them that Commandant Mbembelé did not look favorably on the presence of Christian missionaries in his territory, but he counted on the fact that they wouldn't last long. If they didn't die of some tropical illness, or suffer a timely accident, they would be defeated by exhaustion and frustration. He allowed them to build a small school and a dispensary for the medicines they had brought with them, but he did not permit children to attend classes or the sick to go to the mission. The brothers devoted themselves to teaching good hygiene to the women, until that, too, was forbidden. They lived in isolation, under constant threat, at the whim of the moods of the king and the commandant.

Brother Fernando suspected, through what little news the missionaries were able to send, that Kosongo and Mbembelé financed their reign of terror through contraband. The region was rich in diamonds and other precious stones. There was also uranium, which as yet had not been exploited.

"And don't the authorities do anything about it?" asked Kate.

"Just where do you think you are, lady? Apparently

you don't know how things get done in this part of the world," replied Brother Fernando.

The Bantu men agreed to take them into Kosongo's territory for a sum in money, beer, and tobacco, with two knives thrown in. The remaining provisions were shoved into duffel bags. The *International Geographic* group hid the liquor and cigarettes at the very bottom, for they were more coveted than money and could be used to pay for services and bribes. Canned sardines and peaches, matches, sugar, powdered milk, and soap were also very valuable for trading.

"*Nobody* touches my vodka," Kate threatened.

"What we will need most are antibiotics, malaria pills, and serum for snakebites," said Angie, packing the plane's first-aid kit, which also contained the vial of tranquilizer Mushaha had sent as a sample.

The Bantus overturned their canoes and tipped up the ends on poles to improvise two roofs, beneath which they took their rest after having drunk and sung at the tops of their voices until the early hours. Apparently they feared neither foreigners nor animals. The remaining party, on the other hand, did not rest well. Clutching their weapons and their various bundles, they could not close their eyes for wanting to keep an eye on the "fishermen," who were sleeping the sleep of the dead.

Dawn broke a little after five. The landscape, wrapped in a mysterious fog, resembled a delicate watercolor. While the exhausted foreigners got ready to leave, the Bantus ran up and down the clearing, kicking a cloth ball in a vigorous game of soccer.

Brother Fernando set up a small altar topped with a cross made of two sticks and called everyone to pray. The Bantus came out of curiosity and the others out of courtesy, but the solemnity he lent to his prayers moved everyone, even Kate, who had watched so many different rites in her travels that she was no longer impressed by anything.

They loaded the slim canoes, distributing the weight of passengers and gear as best they could, and left what they couldn't carry in the plane.

"I hope no one comes along while we're gone," Angie said, giving a farewell pat to the side of her *Super Hawk*.

The plane was her only capital in this world, and she was fearful she would be robbed of everything, down to the last screw. "Four days isn't much," she told herself, but her heart shrank, filled with unpleasant presentiments. Four days in that jungle were an eternity.

The group got under way at about eight in the morning. They strung canvas to shield them from the sun, which bore down mercilessly when they had to travel up the middle of the river. While the foreigners were perishing from thirst and heat, besieged by bees and flies, the Bantus were effortlessly paddling against the current, urging one another on with jokes and long swigs of the palm wine they were carrying in plastic containers. They got the wine the simplest way imaginable: they made a V-shaped cut low on the trunk of a palm tree, hung a gourd beneath it, and waited for it to fill with sap, which they then allowed to ferment.

There was the babble of birds in the air and a fiesta of fishes in the water. They saw hippopotamuses— maybe the same family they'd met at the riverbank the first night—and two classes of crocodiles: grays, along with the smaller brown ones. Angie, safe in the canoe, took the opportunity to hurl insults at them. The Bantus tried to catch one of the large ones, knowing the skin would bring a good price, but Angie became hysterical, and her companions were just as reluctant as she to share the crowded canoe with the beast, even with its feet and snout tied. They'd had a chance to appreciate those rows of regenerating teeth and the force of that slashing tail.

A species of dark water snake brushed past one of the canoes and suddenly blew itself up into a bird with white-striped wings and black tail. They watched it as it rose into the air and flew off toward the forest. Later a large shadow passed over their heads and Nadia gave a cry of recognition: It was a crowned eagle. Angie told them that she had once seen a similar bird carry off a gazelle in its claws. White water lilies floated among large, fleshy green leaves, forming islands they had to swing around to avoid getting tangled in roots. Along both banks the vegetation was thick with hanging vines, ferns, roots, and branches. From time to time, there were dots of color in the uniform green of that nature: purple, red, yellow, and pink orchids.

They traveled north for most of the day. The tireless men never varied the rhythm of their paddles, not even in the hottest part of the day, when their passengers were half fainting. Since there was no pause for lunch, they had to be content with crackers, bottled water, and a small amount of sugar. No one wanted sardines; the thought of them turned their stomachs.

About midafternoon, when the sun was still high in the sky but the heat was relenting slightly, one of the Bantu men pointed to the shore. The canoes stopped.

Here the river split into one wide arm that continued north and a narrow channel to the left that led into thick undergrowth. At the entrance to the lesser channel stood something that looked like a scarecrow. It was a life-size wooden statue garbed in raffia, feathers, and strips of hide. The mouth of its gorilla head was open, as if uttering a gruesome scream. Two stones were fitted into the sockets of the eyes. The trunk was studded with nails, and the head was crowned with an incongruous bicycle wheel that served as a kind of sombrero, from which swung bones and dried hands that may have been monkeys' paws. The figure was surrounded by other equally frightening dolls and animal skulls.

"Those are satanic witchcraft dolls!" cried Brother Fernando, making the sign of the cross.

"They *are* a little uglier than the saints in Catholic churches," Kate replied sarcastically.

Joel and Alexander focused their cameras on them.

The terrorized Bantus announced that this was as far as they were going, and although Kate tempted them with more money and cigarettes, they refused to continue. They explained that that macabre altar marked the border of Kosongo's territory. Beyond that lay his domain, and no one entered without his permission. They added that there was a track through the forest that they could follow and reach the village before nightfall. It wasn't very far, they said, only one or two hours, and they would be able to follow the trail by looking for trees slashed by machete. The Bantus drove the noses of their canoes onto the bank and without waiting for instructions began throwing bundles to shore.

Kate paid them part of what they were owed and, with her bad French and the help of Brother Fernando, managed to communicate that in four days they were to come pick them up at this same spot. At that time they would be given the rest of the money and a bonus in cigarettes and canned peaches. The Bantus accepted with fake smiles, stumbled away, climbed into their canoes, and shot off as if pursued by demons.

"What eccentric men!" Kate commented.

"I'm afraid we'll never see them again," Angie added, worried.

"We had better start before it gets dark," said Brother Fernando, slinging his knapsack onto his back and picking up a couple of the duffels.

CHAPTER SIX

THE TRACK THE BANTUS HAD referred to was invisible. The terrain was a quagmire strewn with roots and branches, where feet often sank into a soft pudding of insects, leeches, and worms. Huge rats as big as dogs scurried away at the group's passing. Fortunately, they were wearing boots to midcalf, which at least protected them against snakes. It was so humid that both Alexander and Kate chose to take off their befogged glasses, while Brother Fernando, who saw almost nothing without his, had to clean his lenses every five minutes. In that lush vegetation it was nearly impossible to locate the trees that had been slashed by machetes.

Once again Alexander felt how the tropical climate drained the body and produced a profound indifference in the soul. He missed the clean, invigorating cold of the snowy mountains he climbed with his father and loved so much. He knew that if he felt overwhelmed, his grandmother must be on the verge of a heart attack, but Kate rarely complained. She was not disposed to be defeated by age. She said that people betray their years when they get bent over and make old person sounds: coughing, hawking, creaking, moans. Which was why she always stood very erect and stifled any senior noises.

The group practically felt their way forward as monkeys rained down projectiles from the trees. They had a general idea about the direction they should be heading in, but no notion of how far they were from the village. They suspected even less the kind of reception that awaited them.

They walked for more than an hour, but they made very little headway; this was not terrain in which you could hurry. They had to cross through more than one swamp with water up to the waist. In one of them, Angie took a false step and screamed when she realized that she was sinking in quicksand and that her efforts to free herself were futile. Brother Fernando and Joel held one end of a rifle and she grabbed onto the other end with both hands, and in that way was pulled to firm ground. In the process Angie let go of the duffel she was carrying.

"I lost my pack!" Angie cried when she saw it sinking into the mud.

"That's of no consequence, miss; what matters is

that we got you out," Brother Fernando replied.

"What do you mean, no consequence? My cigarettes and my lipstick are in there!"

Kate heaved a sigh of relief. At least she wouldn't have to smell Angie's delicious tobacco any longer; the temptation was getting unbearable.

They stopped by a small pool to rinse off a little, but they had to resign themselves to mud in their boots. In addition they had the uncomfortable sensation that they were being observed from the impenetrable growth.

"I think someone's spying on us," Kate said finally, unable to bear the tension any longer.

They formed a circle, armed with their reduced arsenal: Angie's revolver and rifle, one machete, and a pair of knives.

"May God protect us," mumbled Brother Fernando, a prayer that was escaping his lips more and more frequently.

After a few minutes, human figures as small as children cautiously emerged from the thicket, the tallest no more that four and a half feet tall. They had yellowish brown skin, nappy hair, wide-set eyes, short legs, long trunks and arms, and flattened noses.

"These must be the famous forest Pygmies," said

Angie, greeting them with a wave.

They wore only minimal breechcloths, except for one whose tattered T-shirt hung to below his knees. They were armed with spears, but they weren't raised threateningly; rather, the men were using them as walking staffs. Two of them were carrying a net rolled onto a pole. Nadia realized that it was identical to the net that had trapped the gorilla where their plane had come down, many miles away. The Pygmies answered Angie's greeting with confident smiles and a few words in French; then they launched into uninterrupted chatter in their own tongue, which no one understood.

"Can you take us to Ngoubé?" Brother Fernando interrupted.

"Ngoubé? *Non! Non!*" the Pygmies exclaimed.

"We have to go to Ngoubé," the missionary insisted.

The man in the T-shirt seemed to be the one best qualified to communicate, because in addition to his limited vocabulary in French, he knew a few words of English. He introduced himself as Beyé-Dokou. Another Pygmy pointed to him and said that he was the *tuma* of their clan, that is, the best hunter. Beyé-Dokou quieted him with a friendly push, but from the satisfied expression on his face he seemed proud of the title. The other men started laughing uproariously, loudly teasing and making fun of him. Any hint of vanity was viewed badly among the Pygmies. Beyé-Dokou sank his head between his shoulders, embarrassed. With difficulty he explained to Kate that they should not go near the village because it was a very dangerous place; they should leave as quickly as possible.

"Kosongo, Mbembelé, Sombe, soldiers," he repeated, and his face reflected his terror.

When the travelers insisted that they must go to Ngoubé at any cost, and that it would be four days before the canoes returned to pick them up, Beyé-Dokou seemed very worried. He consulted for some time with the other men and finally he offered to lead them by a secret route through the jungle back to the place they had left the plane.

"They must be the ones who set the trap," commented Nadia, motioning to the net the two pygmies were carrying.

"And it seems that the idea of going to Ngoubé doesn't suit them at all," commented Alexander.

"I've heard that they are the only humans able to live in these swamps. They move through the jungle by instinct. It may be best for us to go with them, before it's too late," said Angie.

"We're already here, and we will continue to

Ngoubé. Wasn't that what we agreed?" asked Kate.

"To Ngoubé," Brother Fernando repeated.

With eloquent gestures the Pygmies made clear their opinion about the folly of that move, but finally they agreed to guide them. They set down their net beneath a tree, and without further ado took the duffels and knapsacks from the foreigners, threw them over their own shoulders, and started off at a trot through the ferns, so fast that it was nearly impossible to keep up. They were very strong and agile. Each of them was carrying more than sixty pounds, but it didn't hinder them in the least; the muscles of their arms and legs were like reinforced concrete. As the *International Geographic* crew panted along, near fainting from fatigue and heat, the Pygmies, without the least effort, ran with short little steps, feet pointed out like ducks and jabbering all the way.

Beyé-Dokou told them more about the three persons he had mentioned before: King Kosongo, Commandant Mbembelé, and Sombe, whom he described as a terrible sorcerer.

He explained to them that King Kosongo's feet never touched the ground, because if they did, the earth trembled. He said that the king's face was always covered, so no one would see his eyes. Those eyes were so powerful that a single glance could kill from afar. Kosongo never spoke to anyone, because his voice was like thunder: It deafened people and terrorized animals. The king spoke only through The Royal Mouth, a person from his court who had been trained to survive the power of his voice and whose task it was also to taste his food, to prevent the king's being poisoned or harmed by black magic through what he ate. The Pygmy warned them always to keep their head at a level lower than the king's. The correct procedure was to fall facedown and crawl in his presence.

The tiny man in the yellow T-shirt described Mbembelé by aiming an invisible weapon, firing, and falling to the ground as if dead; also by making thrusts with his spear and acting as if he were hacking off hands and feet with a machete or axe. The pantomime could not be clearer. He added that they should never contradict Mbembelé, though it was obvious that the one of the three he feared most was Sombe. Just the name of the sorcerer sent the Pygmies into a state of terror.

The path was not visible, but their small guides had traveled it many times and they had no need to consult the marks on the trees. They passed a clearing in the thick growth where there were other voodoo dolls similar to the ones they'd seen; these, however, were a reddish brown, like iron oxide. As they came closer, they could see that the color came from dried blood. All about the dolls were piles of garbage, animal carcasses, rotted fruit, hunks of cassava, and gourds holding various liquids, perhaps palm wine and other liquors. The stench was unbearable. Brother Fernando crossed himself, and Kate reminded the frightened Joel that he was there to take photographs.

"I hope the blood came from sacrificed animals, not humans," the photographer murmured.

"Village of ancestors," said Beyé-Dokou, pointing to the narrow path that started at the dolls and disappeared into the forest.

He explained that they'd had to make a long detour to reach Ngoubé in order not to pass through the lands of the ancestors, where the spirits of the dead wandered. It was a basic rule of safety: Only a fool or a lunatic would venture there.

"Whose ancestors are they?" Nadia inquired.

Beyé-Dokou struggled to understand the question, but finally with Brother Fernando's help he got the idea.

"Ours," he clarified, pointing to his companions and

using gestures to indicate that the spirits were short.

"Do Kosongo and Mbembelé also stay away from the ghost village of the Pygmies?" Nadia insisted.

"Nobody go there. If the spirits are disturbed, they take revenge. They enter the bodies of the living, they control they will, they cause sickness and suffering, sometimes death," Beyé-Dokou answered.

The Pygmies motioned to the foreigners that they must hurry, because the spirits of animals also come out at night to hunt.

"How do you know if it's the ghost of an animal, not just an ordinary animal?" Nadia asked.

"Because ghost don't have smell of animal. Leopard that smell like antelope, or serpent that smell like elephant, is ghost," he explained.

"Then I guess you need a good sense of smell, or else have to get real close, to tell the difference," Alexander joked.

Beyé-Dokou told them that at one time they hadn't been afraid of the night or the spirits of animals—only those of their ancestors—because they'd been protected by Ipemba-Afua. Kate wanted to know if that was some god, but he corrected her misimpression; he was referring to a sacred amulet that had belonged to their tribe since time immemorial. The way he described it, they understood that it was a human bone that contained a never-ending powder that cured many ills. They had used the powder more times than they could count and through many generations, and it never ran out. Every time they opened the bone, they found it filled with the magical substance. Ipemba-Afua represented the soul of their people, they said; it was their source of health, strength, and good fortune for the hunt.

"Where is it?" asked Alexander.

The Pygmies told them, with tears in their eyes, that Ipemba-Afua had been seized by Mbembelé and was now in Kosongo's power. As long as the king had the amulet, they had no soul; they were at his mercy.

Foreigners and guides entered Ngoubé with the last light of day, when the villagers were beginning to set fires to light the village. They passed some scrawny plantings of cassava, coffee, and banana, a pair of high wood corrals—perhaps for animals—and a string of windowless huts with sagging walls and ruined roofs. A few long-horned cattle were cropping grass, and half-bald chickens, starving dogs, and wild monkeys were poking around among the huts. A few yards farther along, the path widened into a sort of avenue or large central square; there the dwellings were more reputable looking, as they were mud huts with corrugated zinc or straw roofs.

The arrival of the strangers caused a commotion, and within minutes the people of the village had gathered to see what was going on. From their appearance they seemed to be Bantu, like the men in the canoes who had brought them as far as the fork in the river. Women in rags and naked children formed a compact mass on one side of the square, through which four men taller than the other villagers, surely of a different tribe, made their way. They were dressed in ragged army uniforms and outfitted with antiquated rifles and ammunition belts. One was wearing an explorer's pith helmet adorned with feathers, a yellow T-shirt, and plastic sandals; the others were naked to the waist and barefoot. Strips of leopard skin circled their biceps or heads, and rows of ritual scars adorned cheeks and arms. The lines of the scars were raised dots, as if small stones or beads were implanted beneath the skin.

With the appearance of the soldiers, the Pygmies' attitudes changed instantly: The confidence and happy camaraderie they had shown in the forest disappeared in a breath. They dropped their loads to the ground, lowered their heads, and backed away like beaten dogs.

Beyé-Dokou was the only one who dared give a faint wave of good-bye to the foreigners.

The soldiers pointed their weapons at the new arrivals and barked out a few words in French.

"Good evening," Kate said in English; she was at the head of the line and could think of nothing else to say.

The soldiers ignored her outstretched hand. They surrounded the entire group and with the butts of the rifles pushed them against the wall of a hut before the curious eyes of the onlookers.

"Kosongo, Mbembelé, Sombe . . ." shouted Kate.

The men hesitated before the power of those names, and began arguing in their language. They made them wait for what seemed forever while one of them went to ask for instructions.

Alexander noticed that some people were missing hands or ears, and that several of the children who were watching the scene some distance away had terrible sores on their faces. Brother Fernando told him the ulcers were caused by a virus transmitted by flies; he had seen the same thing in the refugee camps of Rwanda.

"They can be cured with soap and water, but apparently they don't have even that here," he added.

"Didn't you say that the missionaries had a

dispensary?" asked Alexander.

"Those sores are a very bad sign, lad. They mean that my brothers aren't here; otherwise they would have healed those children," the missionary replied, deeply concerned.

Much later, when the sky was black, the messenger returned with the order to take the foreigners to the Tree of Words, where matters of government were decided. They were told to pick up their gear and follow.

The crowd fell back to let them through as the group marched across the square that divided the village. In the center was a magnificent tree whose branches spread over the area like an umbrella. Its trunk was nearly nine feet in diameter, and its roots, exposed to the air, fell from the branches like long tentacles to bury themselves in the ground. There the awe-inspiring Kosongo was awaiting them.

The king was on a platform, seated on a large red plush and gilt wood antique armchair. A pair of elephant tusks, on end, stood on either side of the French-style chair, and leopard skins covered the floor. Surrounding the throne were witchcraft dolls and a series of wooden statues with frightening expressions.

Three musicians in blue military uniform jackets, but no trousers or shoes, were beating sticks together. Smoking torches and two bonfires were ablaze, lending the scene a theatrical air.

Kosongo was decked out in a robe embroidered all over with shells, feathers, and unexpected objects like bottle caps, rolls of film, and bullets. The mantle must have weighed at least eighty pounds. He was wearing, in addition, a monumental three-foot-tall hat adorned with four gold horns, symbols of power and courage. Around his neck hung various amulets and necklaces of lions' teeth, and a python skin encircled his waist. A curtain of beads of glass and gold covered his face. A solid gold baton topped with a dried monkey's head served as a scepter, and from that symbol of supreme power dangled a bone carved with delicate designs. From the size and shape, it appeared to be a human tibia. The foreigners deduced that this might well be Ipemba-Afua, the amulet the pygmies had described. The king's fingers were covered with gold rings in the form of various animals, and heavy gold bracelets circled his arms to the elbow. He was as impressive as the sovereigns of England on coronation day, though in a rather different style.

The king's guards and aides stood in a semicircle

around the throne. They, like everyone else in the village, appeared to be Bantu. In contrast, the king was of the same tall tribe as the soldiers. Since he was seated, it was difficult to calculate his size, but he looked enormous, though that, too, could be the effect of the robe and the hat. Commandant Maurice Mbembelé and the sorcerer Sombe were nowhere to be seen.

There were no women or Pygmies in the royal entourage, but behind the male members of the court were some twenty young girls, distinguished from the other inhabitants of Ngoubé by their brightly colored clothes and heavy gold jewelry. In the wavering light of the torches, the yellow metal gleamed against their dark skin. Some of the young women held infants in their arms, and a few small children were playing around their feet. It was easy to deduce that this was the family of the king, and it was striking that the women seemed as submissive as the Pygmies. Apparently their social position provided no sense of pride, only fear.

Brother Fernando informed his fellows that polygamy is common in Africa, and that often the number of wives and children indicates the level of a man's economic power and prestige. In the case of a king, the more children he has, the more prosperous his nation. In this tradition, as in many others, the influence of Christianity and of Western culture had not made much of a dent in local customs. The missionary ventured that Kosongo's women had perhaps not chosen their fate but had been forced to marry him.

The four towering soldiers prodded the foreigners, indicating that they should prostrate themselves before the king. When Kate tried to look up, a blow to her head stopped her immediately. There they lay, swallowing the dust of the square, humiliated and trembling, for long, uncomfortable minutes, until the beating of the musicians' sticks ended and a metallic sound put an end to their waiting. The prisoners dared glance toward the throne: The bizarre monarch was ringing a gold bell.

As the echo of the bell died away, one of the counselors walked forward and the king said something into his ear. That man then spoke to the foreigners in a jumble of French, English, and Bantu to announce, as introduction, that Kosongo had been chosen by God and had a divine mission to govern. The foreigners again buried their noses in the dust, with no desire to express any doubt about that affirmation. They realized that they were listening to The Royal Mouth, just as Beyé-Dokou had described. Then the emissary asked them the purpose of their visit to the domain of the magnificent sovereign Kosongo. His threatening tone left no question in regard to his opinion of their presence. No one answered. The only ones who understood what he'd said were Kate and Brother Fernando, but they were confused. They didn't know the protocol, and didn't want to risk doing something inappropriate; perhaps the question was merely rhetorical, and Kosongo didn't expect an answer.

The king waited a few seconds in the midst of absolute silence, then again rang the bell, which was interpreted by the people as a command. The entire village, except for the Pygmies, began to shout and wave their fists, closing in a circle around the group of visitors. Curiously, their actions did not have the feeling of a spontaneous uprising; it seemed more like a bit of theater executed by bad actors. There was no trace of excitement in the shouting, and some were even laughing when their backs were turned. The soldiers who had firearms crowned the collective demonstration with an unexpected salvo aimed into the air, which produced a stampede in the square. Adults, children, monkeys, dogs, and hens ran to hide as far away as possible. The only persons remaining beneath the tree were the king, his reduced court, his terrorized harem, and the prisoners, still on the ground, arms covering their heads, sure that this was their last moment on earth.

Gradually calm returned to the village. Once the firing had stopped and the noise had faded, The Royal Mouth repeated the question. This time Kate rose to her knees with what little dignity her old bones would allow and, taking care to keep below the level of the temperamental sovereign, as Beyé-Dokou had instructed, she spoke to the intermediary firmly, yet trying not to provoke him.

"We are journalists and photographers," she said, waving vaguely in the direction of her companions.

The king whispered something to his aide, who then repeated his words.

"All of you?"

"No, Your Most Serene Majesty, sir. This woman is owner of the plane that brought us here, and the gentleman with the glasses is a missionary," Kate explained, pointing to Angie and Brother Fernando. And added, before he asked about Nadia and Alexander, "We have come from a great distance to interview your Most Original Majestyness, because your fame has passed far beyond the boundaries of your nation to spread throughout the world."

Kosongo, who seemed to know much more French than The Royal Mouth, focused on the writer.

"What do you mean, old woman?" he asked through his spokesman.

"Outside your country there is great curiosity about your person, Your Most Regal Majesty."

"Why is that?" asked The Royal Mouth.

"You have succeeded in imposing peace, prosperity, and order in this region, Your Most Absolute Highness. News has come that you are a brave warrior; your authority, wisdom, and wealth are well known. They say that you are as powerful as King Solomon of old."

Kate continued her tirade, getting tangled in her words because she hadn't practiced her French in twenty years, and in her ideas, because she wasn't overly confident about her plan. They were, after all, in the twenty-first century; those primitive kings in bad movies who were awed by an opportune eclipse of the sun no longer existed. She supposed that Kosongo was a little behind the times, but he wasn't stupid: It would take more than an eclipse to convince him. It had occurred to her, nevertheless, that he was probably susceptible to adulation, like most men with power. It was not in her character to flatter anyone, but in a long lifetime she had found that you can pay the most ridiculous compliments to a man, and usually he believes them. Her one hope was that Kosongo would swallow her clumsy hook.

Her doubts were soon dissipated, because her tactic of fawning over the king had the hoped-for effect. Kosongo was convinced of his divine origin. For years no one had questioned his power; the life and death of his subjects depended on his whims. He considered it normal that a group of journalists would travel across half the world to interview him; the only strange thing was that they hadn't done so earlier. He decided to receive them as they deserved.

Kate was wondering to herself where all that gold came from; the village was one of the poorest she had ever seen. What other riches lay in the hands of the king? What was the relationship between Kosongo and Commandant Mbembelé? Possibly both of them planned to retire and enjoy their fortunes in a more attractive place than this labyrinth of swamp and jungle. In the meantime, Ngoubé's people lived in misery, with no communication with the outside world, and no electricity, clean water, education, or medicine.

CHAPTER SEVEN

Prisoners of Kosongo

❖

WITH ONE HAND KOSONGO RANG the little gold bell and with the other he directed the villagers, who were still hiding behind huts and trees, to come closer. The attitude of the soldiers changed; they bent down to help the foreigners get to their feet and brought small, three-legged stools for their comfort. The people approached with caution.

"Party! Music! Food!" Kosongo ordered through his Royal Mouth, and indicated to the frightened group of foreigners that they were to take a seat on the stools.

The king's bead-curtained face turned toward Angie. Feeling that she was being examined, she tried to disappear behind her companions, but her bulk was rather too substantial to conceal.

"I think he's looking at me. His gaze doesn't kill, as they say it does, but I feel like he's stripping me with his eyes," Angie whispered to Kate.

"Maybe he wants you for his harem," Kate replied jokingly.

"No way!"

Kate had to admit that though Angie wasn't young anymore, she could hold her own in beauty compared with any of Kosongo's wives. In this village girls were married while still in their early teens, and in Africa the pilot was considered a mature woman. Her tall, voluminous body, however, and her white teeth and lustrous skin, were very attractive. The writer pulled one of her precious bottles of vodka from her backpack and laid it at the feet of the monarch, who was not impressed. With a scornful gesture he authorized his subjects to claim the modest gift. The bottle passed from hand to hand among the soldiers. Then the king took a carton of cigarettes from beneath his mantle, and the soldiers distributed one to each man in the village. The women, who were not considered to be of the same species as the males, were ignored. None were offered to the foreigners. Angie, who was experiencing the symptoms of nicotine withdrawal, was desperate.

The king's wives received no more consideration than the rest of the female population of Ngoubé. A strict old man had the responsibility of keeping them in line, a task for which he kept at hand a slender length of bamboo he did not hesitate to use for whipping their legs whenever it pleased him. Apparently mistreating queens in public was not frowned upon.

Brother Fernando found courage to ask about the missing missionaries, and The Royal Mouth replied that there had never been any missionaries in Ngoubé. He added that no foreigners had visited the village for years, except for an anthropologist who had come to measure the heads of the Pygmies but had beat a fast retreat a few days later because he couldn't bear the climate and the mosquitoes.

"That would have been Ludovic Leblanc," Kate said, and sighed.

She recalled that Leblanc, her archenemy and colleague in the Diamond Foundation, had given her his essay to read, a study on the Pygmies of the equatorial jungle. According to Leblanc, they had the freest and most egalitarian society on earth. Men and women lived in close companionship, the husbands and wives hunting together and equally sharing in the care of the children. There were no hierarchies among them, the only honorific posts being "leader," "healer," and "best hunter," and those positions did not carry power or privilege, only responsibilities. There were no differences between genders or old and young, and the children owed no obedience to the parents. Violence among members of the clan was unknown. They lived in family groups, and no one owned more than anyone else; they produced only what was indispensable for the day's livelihood. There was no incentive to accumulate goods because as soon as someone acquired something, the relatives were entitled to take it. The Pygmies were a fiercely independent people who had not been subjugated even by European colonizers, but in recent times many of them had been enslaved by the Bantus.

Kate was never sure about how much truth was contained in Leblanc's academic writing, but her intuition told her that the pompous professor could be in the right regarding the Pygmies. For the first time, Kate missed him. Arguing with Leblanc was the salt in her life. It kept her in fine fighting form; it wasn't good to spend too much time out of touch with him, or her character might grow soft. The aging writer feared nothing so much as the idea of turning into a harmless little old grandmother.

Brother Fernando was sure that the spokesman was lying about the lost missionaries and persisted with his questions until Angie and Kate reminded him of the proper protocol. It was obvious that the subject annoyed the king. Kosongo seemed to be a time bomb just waiting to explode, and they were in a very vulnerable position.

To honor the visitors, the villagers offered them gourds of palm wine, some leaves that looked like spinach, and a kind of pudding made from cassava. There was also a basket of large rats that had been roasted over the open fire and seasoned with streams of an orange-colored oil obtained from palm seeds. Alexander closed his eyes, thinking nostalgically about the cans of sardines in his knapsack, but a kick from his grandmother jolted him back to reality. It was not prudent to refuse the king's dinner.

"But they're rats, Kate!" he exclaimed, trying to contain his nausea.

"Don't be squeamish. They taste like chicken," she replied.

"That's what you said about the snake in the Amazon, and it wasn't true," her grandson reminded her.

The palm wine turned out to be a disgustingly sweet and nauseating brew that the *International Geographic* group tasted out of courtesy but couldn't swallow. On the other hand, the soldiers and other men of the village gulped it down, drinking until no one was left sober. All attempts to guard the prisoners were abandoned, but they had nowhere to escape to. They were surrounded by jungle, the miasma of the swamps, and the danger of wild animals. The roasted rats and the leaves turned out to be more acceptable than appearances would suggest. The cassava pudding, however, tasted like bread soaked in soapy water, but they were hungry and ate everything down to the last crumb. Nadia limited herself to the bitter spinach, but Alexander surprised himself sucking the leg bones of a rat with great pleasure. His grandmother was right: It did taste like chicken. More specifically, like smoked chicken.

Suddenly Kosongo rang his gold bell again.

"Bring on my Pygmies!" The Royal Mouth shouted to the soldiers, and added for the visitors' benefit: "I have many Pygmies; they are my slaves. They are not human; they live in the jungle like monkeys."

Several drums of different sizes were brought to the plaza, some so large it took two men to carry them. Others had been made from hides stretched over gourds or rusty gasoline tins. At an order from the soldiers, the small group of Pygmies, the same who had brought the foreigners to Ngoubé and who had not joined in earlier, was pushed toward the instruments. The men took their places reluctantly, heads hanging, not daring to disobey.

"They have to play music and dance so their ancestors will lead an elephant to their nets. Tomorrow they will go out to hunt, and they cannot return with empty hands," Kosongo explained through his spokesman.

Beyé-Dokou gave a few tentative thumps, as if to establish the tone and whip up enthusiasm, and then the others followed. The expression on their faces changed; they seemed transfigured. Their eyes shone and their bodies moved in rhythm with their hands as the volume rose and the beat of the drums accelerated. They seemed incapable of resisting the seduction of the music they themselves were creating. Their voices rose in an extraordinary song that undulated on the air like a serpent and then stopped to give way to counter melody. The instruments came alive, competing with each other, connecting, pulsing, animating the night. Alexander calculated that half a dozen percussion orchestras with electric amplifiers could not equal their volume. The Pygmies reproduced the sounds of nature, some as delicate as water rippling over stones or the leaping of gazelles; others deep as the tread of elephants, thunder, or galloping buffaloes. Still others were laments of love, war cries, or moans of pain. The music rose in intensity and beat, reaching a climax, then diminishing until it became a nearly inaudible sigh. The cycles were repeated, never identical, each magnificent, filled with grace and emotion, music only the best jazz players can produce.

At another signal from Kosongo, they brought in the Pygmy women, whom the foreigners had not seen until that moment. They were kept in pens at the entrance to the village. They were all young, dressed only in raffia skirts. They came forward slowly, dragging their feet, humbled, as the guards shouted orders to them and threatened them. When the musicians saw the women, they froze; the drums stopped abruptly and, for a few instants, only the echoes vibrated through the jungle.

The guards lifted their sticks and the women shrank, huddling together to protect themselves. Immediately the instruments began to sound with new vigor. Then before the helpless gaze of the visitors, a mute dialogue began between the women and musicians. As the men pounded the drums, expressing the whole scale of human emotions, from anger and pain to love and nostalgia, the women danced in a circle, swinging their raffia skirts, lifting their arms, pounding the ground with their bare feet, answering with their movements and song the anguished call of their companions. The spectacle was one of primitive and painful intensity. It was unbearable.

Nadia hid her face in her hands; Alexander held her tight because he was afraid that his friend would leap into the center of the square and try to put an end to that degrading dance. Kate came over to warn them not to make a false move, because it could be fatal. They only had to look at Kosongo to understand what she was saying: He seemed possessed. Still seated on the French chair that served as his throne, he was shaking to the rhythm of the drums as if jolted by an electric current. The trinkets on his robe and hat were chattering, his feet were keeping time with the drums, and his jerking arms set his gold bracelets jangling. Several members of his court, and even the drunken soldiers, began to dance, and after them, the rest of the villagers. Soon there was a pandemonium of people twisting and jumping around.

The collective dementia ceased as suddenly as it had begun. At a sign that only they perceived, the musicians stopped beating their drums, and the pathetic dance of their companions was cut short. As a group, the women retreated toward the pens. The moment the drums were silenced, Kosongo's erratic behavior ended; his subjects, too, returned to normal. Only the sweat running down his naked arms recalled the king's frenzy. It was then the foreigners noticed that ritual scars like those of the soldiers disfigured his arms, and that like them he wore strips of leopard skin tied around his biceps. His courtesans hastened to settle the heavy mantle around his shoulders and to straighten his hat, which had shifted to one side.

The Royal Mouth explained to the foreigners that if they did not leave soon they would be present during *ezenji*, the dance of the dead, which is performed at funerals and executions. *Ezenji* was also the name of the great spirit. As might be expected, this news did not meet with enthusiasm. Before anyone dared ask details, the same person told them, speaking for the king, that they would be escorted to their "chambers."

Four men lifted the platform holding the royal chair-throne and bore Kosongo off toward his compound, followed by his wives carrying the two elephant tusks and corralling their children. The throne bearers had drunk so much that the heavy chair swayed dangerously.

Kate and her friends picked up their bundles and followed two Bantus equipped with torches, who went before them to light the path. They were led by a soldier with a leopard armband and a rifle. The effect of the palm wine and the frenzied dance had put the men in a good humor; they were laughing, joking, and slapping one another on the back. But their mood did not calm the foreigners because it was obvious that they were being treated like prisoners.

The so-called chambers turned out to be a rectangular, straw-roofed, mud building located at the far end of the village, at the very edge of the jungle. Two holes in the walls served as windows, and the entrance was a larger opening with no door. The men with the torches stepped inside to light the interior and, to the revulsion of those who were going to have to spend the night there, thousands of cockroaches scurried across the floor toward the corners.

"Cockroaches are the oldest creatures in the world; they've existed for more than three hundred million years," said Alexander.

"That doesn't make them any more agreeable," Angie pointed out.

"Cockroaches are harmless," Alexander added, although he wasn't sure whether that was true.

"So what about snakes?" Joel asked.

"Pythons don't attack in the dark," joked Kate.

"What is that awful smell?" Alexander asked.

"It could be rat urine or bat excrement," Brother Fernando clarified in a conversational tone; he had run into similar situations in Rwanda.

Alexander laughed. "It's always a treat to travel with you, Grandmother."

"Don't call me Grandmother! If you don't like the

accommodations, go to the Sheraton."

"I'm dying for a smoke!" moaned Angie.

"This is your chance to give it up," Kate replied, without much conviction, because she was badly missing her old pipe.

One of the Bantus lighted other torches placed around the walls, and the soldier ordered them not to come out until morning. If they had any doubts about his words, the threatening gesture with his weapon dissipated that.

Brother Fernando wanted to know if there was a latrine nearby, and the soldier laughed; he found the idea amusing. When the missionary insisted, the tall African lost patience and pushed him with the butt of his rifle, knocking him to the ground. Kate, who was used to commanding respect, intervened decisively by stepping in front of the aggressor and, before he could give her the same treatment, placing a can of peaches in his hand. The man took the bribe and left. After a few minutes, he returned with a plastic pail and handed it to Kate with no further explanation. That battered receptacle would function as indoor plumbing.

"What do those leopard skin ties and scars on their arms represent?" Alexander queried. "All the soldiers have them."

"Too bad we can't get in touch with Leblanc; I'm

sure he could give us an explanation," said Kate.

"I think it means that those men belong to the Brotherhood of the Leopard," Angie told them. "That's a secret society that exists in several African countries. They recruit their members while they're teenagers and mark them with those scars so they can be recognized anywhere. They're mercenaries; they fight and die for money. Its members have a reputation for brutality. They take an oath that they will help one another all through their lifetimes and kill their mutual enemies. They don't have families, or ties of any kind, except for their brothers in the society."

"Negative solidarity," Brother Fernando amplified. "To them it means that anything any one of them does is justified, no matter how horrible. That's the opposite of positive solidarity. In that people join together to build and plant and provide food and protect the weak . . . all to better their conditions. Negative solidarity is a brotherhood of bullies, and of war and violence and crime."

"I see that we've fallen into very good hands," said Kate, who was exhausted.

The group prepared to spend a bad night, watched from the door by two Bantu guards armed with machetes. The soldier left. As soon as they tried to get comfortable on the ground, using their packs as pillows, the cockroaches returned and crawled all over them. They resigned themselves to little feet probing into their ears, scrabbling across their eyelids, and poking beneath their clothing. Angie and Nadia tied kerchiefs around their heads to prevent the insects from nesting in their long hair.

"You don't find snakes where there are cockroaches," said Nadia.

The idea had just occurred to her, but it had the desired result: Joel, who up to that moment had been a bundle of nerves, calmed down as if by magic, happy to have the cockroaches as bedfellows.

During the night, when her companions finally surrendered to sleep, Nadia decided she had to do something. The others were so fatigued that they were able to rest at least for a few hours—despite the rats, the cockroaches, and the menacing proximity of Kosongo's men. Nadia, however, was too upset by the spectacle of the Pygmies to be able to sleep, and so she decided to find out what was going on in those pens the women had returned to after their dance. She took off her boots and picked up a flashlight. The two guards sitting outside with machetes across their knees would be no obstacle, for she had spent three years practicing the art of invisibility learned from Indians in the Amazon. The body-painted People of the Mist silently disappeared by blending into the surrounding nature, moving with a lightness and a mental concentration so profound that it could be sustained for a brief period only. That "invisibility" had helped Nadia out of trouble on more than one occasion, which was why she practiced so often. She went in and out of her classes unnoticed by other students or the teachers, and later no one remembered whether she had been in school that day. She rode the crowded subways in New York without being seen, and to test it she would stand a few inches from a fellow passenger and stare straight into his eyes, without getting a reaction. Kate, with whom Nadia lived, was the main victim of this tenacious training; she was never sure whether the girl was there or whether she had dreamed her.

Nadia didn't want to take Borobá with her, so she ordered him to stay in the hut and keep quiet. Then she took several deep breaths to quiet her nerves completely, and concentrated on becoming invisible. When she was ready, she moved in a nearly hypnotic state. She stepped over the bodies of her sleeping friends without touching them and slipped toward the exit. Outside, the guards, bored and drunk from the palm wine, had decided to take turns standing guard. One of them was propped against the wall, snoring, and the other was peering into the deep black of the jungle, a little frightened because he feared the ghosts of the forest. Nadia stepped into the doorway; the man turned toward her, and for a moment their eyes met. The guard seemed to sense her presence, but that impression was immediately erased and he yawned a great yawn. He stood in place, fighting sleep, his machete abandoned on the ground as the slender silhouette of the girl moved past him.

Nadia crossed through the village in the same ethereal state, unseen by the few people still awake. She passed right by the torches lighting the mud buildings of the royal compound. A sleepless monkey leaped from a tree and landed at her feet, causing her to return to her body for a few instants, but she quickly concentrated and continued forward. She felt weightless, floating, as she approached the pens, two rectangular enclosures constructed from poles driven into the ground and lashed together with vines and strips of hide. One section of each pen was covered by a straw roof; the other half was open to the sky. The gate was closed with a heavy bar that could be opened only from the outside. No one was on guard.

Testing the wall of the palisade with her hands, Nadia walked around the two pens, not daring to turn on the flashlight. She found a strong, high fence, but a determined person could use the knots on the wood and tangles in the vines to climb it. She wondered why the Pygmies hadn't escaped. After she had circled the area a couple of times and made sure that no one was about, she decided to lift the bar on one of the gates. In her invisible state she had to be very cautious in her movements; she couldn't do the things she normally could. She would have to emerge from her trance to push up the heavy bar.

The sounds of the forest filled the night: voices of animals and birds, murmurings in the trees and sighs on the ground. Nadia thought that the people of the village had good reason not to venture out at night; it would be easy to attribute those sounds to supernatural beings. Her efforts to open the gate were far from silent because the wood creaked loudly. A few dogs trotted toward her, barking, but Nadia spoke to them in their language and they quieted immediately. It seemed to her that she heard a baby crying, but that, too, stopped after a few seconds. Again she pushed the bolt with her shoulder; it was heavier than she had imagined. At last she was able to lift the bar from the supports; she pushed open the gate and slipped inside.

By then her eyes had adapted to the night, and she could see that she was in a kind of courtyard. With no idea of what she might find, she moved quietly toward the roofed area, picturing how she would escape in case of danger. She decided that she couldn't keep walking around in the dark, and after a brief hesitation she switched on the flashlight. The beam of light revealed a scene so unexpected that Nadia screamed. Some fourteen or fifteen tiny figures were lined up along the far end of the enclosure, their backs against the palisade. Her first thought was that they were children, but immediately she realized they were the same women who had danced for Kosongo. They seemed as terrified as she was but they didn't utter a sound; all they did was stare at the intruder with bulging eyes.

"Shhh," said Nadia, putting a finger to her lips. "I'm not going to hurt you. I'm a friend," she added in Portuguese, her native language in Brazil, and then repeated the words in every language she knew.

The prisoners didn't understand most of what she said but they perceived her intentions. One of them stepped forward, although still in a crouch with her face hidden, and blindly reached out with one arm. Nadia approached slowly and touched her. The Pygmy drew back, frightened, but then dared to peek out of the corner of her eye. She must have been satisfied with the young foreigner's face, because she smiled. Nadia held out her hand again, and the woman did the same; their fingers laced together, and that physical contact became the most elemental form of communication.

"Nadia, Nadia," the girl introduced herself, tapping her chest.

"Jena," the other replied.

Soon all the women were standing around Nadia, looking her over with curiosity as they whispered and laughed. Once they had discovered the shared language of patting and miming, the rest was easy. The Pygmies explained that they had been separated from their men, whom Kosongo forced to hunt elephants—not for the meat but for the tusks, which he sold to smugglers. The king had another clan of slaves who worked a diamond mine a little farther north. He had amassed a fortune. The rewards for the hunters were cigarettes, a little food, and the right to see their families for brief periods of time. When the supply of ivory or diamonds fell short, Commandant Mbembelé intervened. He dealt out a variety of punishments: The most bearable was death; the most horrible was losing their children, whom he sold as slaves to the smugglers. Jena added that there were very few elephants left in the forest, and that the Pygmies had to go farther and farther afield to hunt. There weren't that many men in the tribe, and the women couldn't help them as they had always done. When the elephants grew scarce, the fate of their children was placed in jeopardy.

At first Nadia wasn't sure she had understood. She had always thought that slavery ended some time ago, but the women's pantomime was very clear. Afterward Kate would confirm that there were still slaves in some countries. The Pygmies were considered exotic creatures, and they were bought to perform degrading tasks, or, should they be more fortunate, to entertain the wealthy or be exhibited in circuses.

The prisoners told Nadia that they were doing all the work in Ngoubé—planting, carrying water, cleaning, even building the huts. The one thing they wanted was to be reunited as families and go back to the jungle, where they had lived as a free people for thousands of years. Nadia demonstrated how they could climb the palisade and escape, but they answered her, with gestures, that their children were kept in the other pen, looked after by a couple of grandmothers, and they couldn't leave without them.

"Where are your husbands?" Nadia asked.

Jena told her that they lived in the forest and had permission to visit the village only at the times they brought meat, skins, or ivory. Their husbands, they said, were the musicians who played the drums during Kosongo's fiesta.

CHAPTER EIGHT

The Sacred Amulet

◈

AFTER TELLING THE PYGMIES good-bye and promising to help them, Nadia went back to the hut the same way she'd come, utilizing the art of invisibility. When she got there she found there was only one guard and, thanks to the palm wine, he was snoring like a baby, which was an unexpected break. She slipped silently as a squirrel over to Alexander, waked him—keeping her hand over his mouth—and in few words told him what had happened in the pen where the slaves were kept.

"It's horrible, Jaguar. We have to do something."

"What, for example?"

"I don't know. They used to live in the forest, and in those days they had normal relations with the people of this village. That was when there was a queen named Nana-Asante, who was from another tribe. She came from afar, and the people believed that she had been sent by the gods. She was also a healer who knew all about medicinal plants and exorcisms. The women told me that there used to be broad tracks through the forest beat down by the feet of hundreds of elephants, but that now there are very few animals left, and the jungle has swallowed up those trails. The Pygmies became slaves when their magic amulet was taken from them, which is what Beyé-Dokou had told us before."

"Do you know where it is?"

"It's that carved bone we saw hanging from Kosongo's scepter," Nadia explained.

They talked a while, discussing different ideas, each more risky than the last. Finally they agreed that as a first step they needed to recover the amulet and give it back to the tribe in order to restore their confidence and courage. Then maybe the Pygmies would be able to figure out some way to free their wives and their children.

"If we get the amulet, I'll go look for Beyé-Dokou in the forest," said Alexander.

"You'll get lost."

"My totemic animal will help me. The jaguar knows how to find his way wherever he is, and can see in the dark," Alexander replied.

"I'm going with you."

"That's taking unnecessary chances, Eagle. If I go alone, I can move more freely."

"We can't be apart. Remember what Má Bangesé told us in the market: If we're separated we'll die."

"And you believe that?"

"Yes. The vision we had is a warning: Somewhere a three-headed monster is waiting for us."

"There are no three-headed monsters, Eagle."

"As the shaman Walimai would say, 'Maybe yes and maybe no,'" she replied.

"How are we going to get the amulet?"

"Borobá and I will do it," said Nadia with great assurance, as if it were the simplest thing in the world.

The monkey had an enormous talent for stealing, which had been a real problem back in New York. Nadia spent much of her time returning objects the little monkey had brought her as gifts. Now, however, that bad habit could be a blessing. Borobá was tiny, quiet, and very skillful with his hands. The hard part would be to find out where the amulet was kept, and to get past the guards. Jena had told Nadia that the talisman was in the king's hut; she had seen it when she went there to clean.

That night the villagers were drunk and vigilance was at a minimum. They had seen very few armed soldiers, only those of the Brotherhood of the Leopard, but there could be others. They didn't know how many

men Mbembelé had under his command, but the fact
that the commandant hadn't appeared during the fiesta
the previous night might mean that he wasn't in
Ngoubé. They had to act at once, they decided.

"Kate isn't going to like this at all, Jaguar.
Remember, we promised her that we wouldn't get into
any trouble," said Nadia.

"We're already in pretty serious trouble. I'll leave her
a note so she'll know where we are. Are you afraid?"
Alexander asked.

"I'm afraid to go with you, but I'm more afraid to
stay here."

"Put on your boots, Eagle. We need a flashlight,
extra batteries, and at least one knife. The jungle is
crawling with snakes, so I think we should take a vial
of snakebite serum. Do you think we can borrow
Angie's revolver?" Alex wondered.

"Are you planning to kill someone, Jaguar?"

"Of course not!"

"Well then?"

"All right, Eagle. We won't take weapons."
Alexander sighed with resignation.

The friends collected the things they needed,
moving stealthily among the packs and bundles of their
companions. As they were looking for the snakebite

serum in Angie's first-aid kit, they saw the tranquilizer, and on an impulse, Alexander put that into his pocket.

"What do you want that for?" Nadia asked.

"I don't know, but it might be useful," Alexander replied.

Nadia left first, crossing unseen the short distance illuminated by the torch at the door, and ran to hide in the shadows. From there she meant to attract the guards' attention to give Alexander a chance to follow, but she saw that the one guard was still sleeping and the other hadn't returned. It was a piece of cake for Alexander and Borobá to join her.

The king's mud-and-straw compound was composed of several huts, and it gave the impression of being only temporary. For a monarch covered in gold from head to foot, with a sizeable harem and with Kosongo's supposed divine powers, the "palace" was suspiciously modest. Alexander and Nadia deduced that the king did not intend to grow old in Ngoubé, and for that reason had not constructed something more elegant and comfortable. Once the supplies of ivory and diamonds were fully depleted, he would go as far away as possible to enjoy his fortune.

The area of his harem was encircled by another

pole-and-vine fence, along which, every thirty feet or so, torches had been mounted to keep it well lighted. The torches were sticks wrapped with resin-soaked rags that gave off thick black smoke and a penetrating odor. In front of the fence was a larger building decorated with black geometric designs and featuring an entrance wider and taller than ordinary. That suggested to Alexander and Nadia that this dwelling housed the king, since the opening would allow the throne-carriers to pass through with the platform Kosongo used to travel outside his quarters. Surely the taboo against his feet touching ground did not apply inside his compound. In private, Kosongo must walk on his own two feet, show his face, and speak without need for an intermediary, like any normal person. A short distance away was another long, squat, windowless building; this one was connected to the king's hut by a straw-roofed passageway, and was possibly the barracks for his soldiers.

Two Bantu guards armed with rifles were patrolling the area. Alexander and Nadia observed them for a period of time and came to the conclusion that Kosongo did not fear being attacked, because the guard system was a joke. These soldiers, still feeling the effect of the palm wine, were staggering as they made their rounds, and they stopped to smoke whenever it struck their fancy. Every time they met, they paused to talk. The two young people even watched them drink from a bottle that possibly contained more liquor. They didn't see any soldiers of the Brotherhood of the Leopard, which made them feel a little better since they were much more intimidating than the Bantus. However, just the thought of going into the building, not knowing what they would find inside, was sobering.

"You wait here, Jaguar. I'll go first. I'll hoot like an owl to let you know when it's time to send in Borobá," Nadia said.

Alexander didn't care for the plan, but he couldn't come up with anything better. Nadia knew how to move around without being seen, and no one would notice Borobá; the village was swarming with monkeys. With his heart in his throat, Alexander sent his friend off and watched as she immediately disappeared. He made a conscious effort to see her, and for a few seconds was successful, though she looked like a veil floating through the night. Despite his edginess, Alexander couldn't help but smile when he witnessed how effective her gift of invisibility was.

Nadia chose a time when the guards were smoking to go to one of the windows of the king's residence. It was no trouble at all to climb to the wide sill and from there look inside. It was dark, but some light from the torches and the moon filtered in through the windows, which were simple openings without glass or shutters. When she saw no one was there, she slipped inside.

The guards finished their cigarettes and made another complete circle of the royal compound. Finally the screech of an owl broke Alexander's terrible tension. He set down Borobá, and the little monkey shot off in the direction of the window where he had last seen his mistress. For several minutes that were as long as hours, nothing happened. Then, as if by magic, Nadia appeared by his side.

"What happened?" asked Alex, forcing himself not to put his arms around her.

"Easy as pie. Borobá knows what to do."

"That means you found the amulet."

"Kosongo must be in the other building with one of his wives. A few men were sleeping on the ground, and others were playing cards. The throne, the platform, the mantle, the hat, the scepter, and the two elephant tusks were there. I also saw some coffers; I suppose that's where he keeps his gold ornaments," Nadia explained.

"And the amulet?"

"It was with the scepter, but I couldn't get it because I'd lost my invisibility. Borobá will do it."

"How?"

Nadia pointed to the window, where Alexander saw billowing black smoke.

"I set fire to the royal mantle," said Nadia.

Almost immediately they heard a confusion of yells; the guards who had been inside came running out, as did several soldiers from the barracks. Soon the whole village was awake, and the area was crowded with people running with pails of water to put out the fire. Borobá took advantage of the confusion to grab the amulet and leap out the window. Instants later he joined Nadia and Alexander, and all three faded off in the direction of the forest.

Beneath the cupola of the treetops, the darkness was nearly absolute. Despite the jaguar's night vision, which Alexander had invoked, it was almost impossible to make any forward progress. It was the hour of the serpents and poisonous insects, of wild beasts on the prowl, but the most immediate danger was of stumbling into a bog and being swallowed up by the mud.

Alexander switched on his flashlight and took stock of their surroundings. He wasn't afraid of being seen from the village because of the dense vegetation, but he was worried about using up the batteries. They plunged through the thick growth, fighting roots and vines, skirting pools of water, tripping over invisible obstacles, enveloped in the constant murmurings of the jungle.

"Well, what do we do now?" asked Alexander.

"Wait for daylight, Jaguar. We can't keep going in this darkness. What time is it?"

"Almost four," the youth replied, consulting his watch.

"It will be light soon, and then we can see where we're going. I'm hungry. I couldn't eat the rats from dinner," said Nadia.

Alexander laughed. "If Brother Fernando were here he would say, 'God will provide.'"

They made themselves as comfortable as possible in a nest of ferns. The humidity soaked their clothing, they were pricked with thorns, and bugs crawled all over them. They heard the *swish* of animals brushing past them, the beating of wings, the heavy breath of the earth. After their adventure in the Amazon, Alexander had never gone exploring without a cigarette lighter; he had learned that striking stones together was not the quickest way to start a fire. That night they tried to start a small bonfire to dry out a little and keep any animals at a distance, but they couldn't find any dry sticks, and after a few attempts they gave up.

"This place is filled with ghosts," said Nadia.

"You believe in ghosts?" asked Alexander.

"Yes, but I'm not afraid of them. You remember Walimai's wife? She was a friendly spirit."

"That was in the Amazon. We don't know what they're like here. There must be a reason why people are afraid of them," said Alexander.

"If you're trying to scare me, you've succeeded," Nadia replied.

Alexander put an arm around his friend's shoulders and cradled her against his chest, trying to make her feel warm and safe. That gesture, once so natural between them, was charged with new meaning.

"Walimai was finally reunited with his wife," Nadia said.

"He died?"

"Yes, now they're both living in the same world."

"How do you know that?"

"You remember when I fell off that cliff and broke my shoulder in the Forbidden Kingdom? Walimai kept me company until you got there with Tensing and Dil Bahadur. When he appeared at my side, I knew that he was a ghost and able to move about in this world, and in others."

"He was a good friend. When you needed him you could whistle, and he always came," Alexander remembered.

"If I need him, he will come now, just as he came to help me in the Forbidden Kingdom. Spirits can travel great distances," Nadia assured him.

Despite their fear and discomfort, Alex and Nadia soon began to nod; they had not slept for twenty-four hours, and had experienced a multitude of emotions since Angie Ninderera's airplane crash-landed. They didn't know how many minutes they'd rested, or how many snakes and other animals had brushed past them, before they were jolted awake. Borobá was pulling their hair with both hands and screeching with terror. It was still dark. Alexander switched on the flashlight, and its beam fell on a black face almost on top of his. Both the creature and he yelled and fell back. The flashlight rolled on the ground, and it was several seconds before Alexander found it. During that moment Nadia had time to react and grab Alexander's arm, whispering that he should keep still. They felt an enormous hand blindly exploring them, and then suddenly it seized

Alexander by his shirt and shook him unmercifully. He switched on the flash again but did not aim it directly at his attacker. In the shadows, they recognized a gorilla.

"*Tempo kachi*, may happiness be yours . . ."

This greeting from the Forbidden Kingdom was the first and only thing that came to Alexander's mind; he was too startled to think. Nadia, on the other hand, made her greeting in the language of the monkeys, because even before she could see, she had recognized what had startled them by the warmth of the body and the breath of newly cut grass. It was the gorilla they had rescued from the trap some days before. As she had then, she had her tiny offspring clasped against the harsh hair of her belly, and she was observing them through curious and intelligent eyes. Nadia wondered how she had gotten here; she must have traveled many miles through the forest, something unusual for those animals.

The gorilla dropped Alexander and put her hand to Nadia's face, pushing her a little, softly, like a caress. Smiling, the girl returned the greeting with a push of her own that did not budge the gorilla an inch but did establish a kind of dialogue. The animal turned her back to them and walked a few steps, then she returned and, again pushing her face close to theirs, uttered a few quiet grunts and, without warning, delicately nibbled Alexander's ear.

"What does she want?" he asked with alarm.

"For us to follow her. She wants to show us something."

They did not have to go far. Suddenly the animal gave a leap and climbed to a kind of nest among the tree branches. Alexander aimed the flashlight toward it and was rewarded with a chorus of unsettling grunts. He switched it off immediately.

"There are several gorillas in this tree, it must be a family," said Nadia.

"That means there's a male and several females with young. The male could be dangerous."

"If our friend has brought us here, it's because we're welcome."

"What do we do now? I don't know what the protocol is between humans and gorillas in a situation like this," Alexander joked nervously.

They waited, motionless, beneath the huge tree. Gradually the grunting stopped. Exhausted, they sat down among the roots of the enormous tree, with Borobá clinging to Nadia and trembling with fear.

"We can sleep in peace; we're protected here. The

gorilla wants to repay us for the favor we did her," Nadia assured Alexander.

"Do you believe that animals have those kinds of emotions, Eagle?" Alexander was doubtful.

"Why not? Animals talk among themselves, they form families, they love their young, they band into societies, they have memories. Borobá is smarter than most of the people I know," Nadia replied.

"On the other hand, my dog, Poncho, is pretty stupid."

"Not everyone has Einstein's brain, Jaguar."

"Poncho definitely doesn't." Alexander smiled.

"But Poncho *is* one of your best friends. There's friendship among animals, too."

These friends slept as deeply as if they were in a featherbed. The proximity of the great apes gave them a sense of complete safety; they couldn't be better protected.

A few hours later, they awakened with no idea of where they were. Alexander looked at his watch and realized that they'd slept longer than they'd intended; it was after seven. The heat of the sun was drawing moisture from the ground, and the jungle, wrapped in warm fog, felt like a Turkish bath. The two friends jumped up and looked around them. The tree of the gorillas had been vacated, and for a minute they had doubts about what had happened the night before. Maybe it was just a dream, but no: There were the nests among the branches, and some tender bamboo tips, the gorillas' favorite food, had been left by their sides as gifts. And if that weren't enough, they realized that several pairs of black eyes were observing them from the thick undergrowth around them. The presence of the gorillas was so close and so palpable that they didn't have to see them to know they were watching.

"*Tempo kachi,*" Alexander said as good-bye.

"Thank you," said Nadia in the language of Borobá.

A long, hoarse roar answered them from the impenetrable green of the forest.

"I think we can take that as a sign of friendship," Nadia said, laughing.

In the village of Ngoubé, dawn announced itself with a mist as thick as smoke, which drifted in through the uncovered door and windows. Despite all the discomforts of the hut, Kate, Angie, and Brother Fernando had slept deeply, with no idea that there had been a fire scare in one of the royal huts. Kosongo had had little to complain about, however, since the flames were doused immediately. When the smoke cleared, it was discovered that the fire had begun in the royal mantle—which was interpreted as a very bad omen—and spread to the leopard skins, which flared up like dry tinder, causing the dense smoke. The prisoners knew nothing of this until several hours later because their hut was at the far end of the village

The first rays of the sun sifted through the straw roof, and in the light of dawn the friends were able to examine their surroundings: a long, narrow hut with thick walls of dark mud. On one of the walls, apparently scratched with the tip of a knife, was the calendar of the preceding year. On another wall they saw verses from the New Testament and a crude wooden cross.

"This is the mission, I'm sure of it," said Brother Fernando emotionally.

"How do you know?" asked Kate.

"I have no doubt. Look at this," he said.

From his knapsack he took a paper that had been folded several times and smoothed it out carefully. It was a pencil drawing sent by the missionaries who had disappeared. Prominent were the central square of the village, the Tree of Words and Kosongo's throne, huts, animal pens, a larger building marked as the king's quarters, and another used as barracks for the soldiers. The drawing showed the mission at the exact spot where they were being held.

"See, this is where they had the school and looked after the sick. There should be a garden nearby, which they planted, and a well."

"Why would they want a well when it rains here every two minutes?" Kate wondered. "There's water to spare all around us."

"They didn't dig it; it was already here. They put quotation marks around the word, as if it were something special. I always thought that was very strange."

"I wonder what happened to them?" Kate said.

"I'm not leaving here until I find out. I have to see Commandant Mbembelé," Brother Fernando said with determination.

For breakfast the guards brought them a stalk of bananas and a pitcher of milk swimming with flies, then returned to their posts at the entrance, in that way notifying the foreigners that they still were not to go outside. Kate pulled off a banana and turned to give it to Borobá. That was when she realized that Alexander, Nadia, and the little monkey were not with them.

Kate became frantic when she found that her grandson and Nadia were not in the hut with the rest of the group, and even more alarmed that no one had seen them since the night before.

"Maybe the young people went for a walk . . ." Brother Fernando suggested without much conviction.

Kate went running out as if she were possessed, before the guard at the door could stop her. Outside, the village was coming to life. Children and a few women were moving around, but there were no men to be seen; no one was working. In the distance they saw the Pygmy women who had danced the night before. Some were going to the river for water; others were headed for the huts of the Bantus or on their way to the fields. Kate ran to ask about Alexander and Nadia, but she couldn't communicate with them, or else they didn't want to answer. She went through the village calling the names of her grandson and Nadia, but she didn't see them anywhere; all she achieved was to stir up the hens and attract the attention of a couple of the soldiers of Kosongo's guard who were beginning their round at that moment. Without a break in stride, they took her by the arms and literally carried her toward the compound of royal huts.

"They have Kate!" screamed Angie, who was watching from a distance.

She tucked her revolver into her waistband, picked up her rifle, and waved to the others to follow her. They should be acting like guests, she said, not prisoners. The group pushed aside the two guards at the door and ran off in the direction in which the writer had disappeared.

By that time, the soldiers had pushed Kate to the ground and would have started beating her had they not been interrupted by her friends, who streamed in shouting in Spanish, English, and French. The foreigners' bold behavior confused the soldiers; they were not used to being disobeyed. There was a law in Ngoubé that no one could touch one of Mbembelé's soldiers. Even if this happened by accident the punishment was a beating; when it was intentional the cost was a life.

"We want to see the king!" demanded Angie, backed by her companions.

Brother Fernando helped Kate up, but a sharp cramp in her ribcage kept her from fully straightening. She thumped her chest a couple of times, and then was able to get her breath.

They had ended up in a large mud hut with a floor of tamped-down earth, bare of furniture. On the walls were two mounted leopard heads, and in a corner an altar covered with voodoo fetishes. In another corner, on a red carpet, sat a refrigerator and a television, symbols of wealth and modernity, though totally useless since there was no electricity in Ngoubé. The room had two doors and there were openings in the walls to let in a little light.

The sound of voices outside caused the soldiers to snap to attention. The foreigners turned to see a man with the look of a gladiator make his entrance through one of the doors. They had no doubt that this was the famous Maurice Mbembelé. He was very tall and muscular, with the build of a weight lifter: enormous shoulders and a thick neck; prominent cheekbones; thick, well-defined lips; a boxer's crooked nose; and shaved head. They couldn't see his eyes because he was wearing mirrored sunglasses, which gave him a particularly sinister appearance. He was clad in army trousers, boots, and a wide, black leather belt, but his torso was bare. He showed the scars of the Brotherhood of the Leopard and wore a strip of leopard skin on each arm. He was accompanied by two soldiers nearly as tall as he.

When she saw the commandant's powerful muscles, Angie was wide-mouthed with admiration. Her fury dissolved in an instant, and she felt as flustered as a schoolgirl. Kate realized that she was about to lose her best ally, and stepped forward.

"Commandant Mbembelé, I presume?" she asked.

The man did not answer; he merely observed the group of foreigners with an inscrutable expression, almost as if he were wearing a mask.

"Commandant, two of our group are missing," Kate announced.

That news was received with an icy silence.

"Two young people, my grandson, Alexander, and his friend Nadia," Kate added.

"We want to know where they are," Angie put in, no longer struck dumb by passion.

"They can't have gone very far; they must be in the village," Kate babbled.

She had the sensation that she was sinking into a quagmire; she was unsteady on her feet and her voice trembled. The silence became unbearable. A long minute passed before they heard the firm voice of the commandant.

"The guards who were so careless will be punished."

That was it. He turned on his heel and left the same way he had come, followed by his two personal guards and those who had manhandled Kate. They were laughing and talking as they left. Brother Fernando and Angie caught part of their joke: The white boy and girl who had escaped were really stupid; they would die in the forest, devoured by wild beasts or by ghosts.

Seeing that no one had an eye on them or even seemed interested in them, Kate and the remaining members of the party went back to the hut they had been assigned to.

"Those kids have just vanished. They're always causing me problems. I swear they're going to pay for this!" Kate groaned, tearing at the short gray clumps of hair that crowned her head.

"Don't swear, woman. We should pray instead," Brother Fernando scolded.

He knelt down among the cockroaches that were calmly moving about the floor and began to pray. No one joined him; they were too busy speculating and suggesting plans.

Angie believed that the sensible thing to do was negotiate with the king to provide them a boat, the only way to leave the village. Joel thought Commandant Mbembelé was in charge of the village, not the king, and that since he showed no sign of willingness to help them, the best idea might be to ask the Pygmies to lead them back along the secret forest trails that only they knew. As for Kate, she had no intention of going anywhere before the two young people returned.

At that point Brother Fernando, who was still on his knees, broke in to show them the piece of paper he had found on one of their packs as he knelt to pray. Kate tore it from his hand and ran to one of the windows where there was light.

"It's from Alexander!"

In a faltering voice the writer read the brief message from her grandson: "Nadia and I are trying to help the Pygmies. Keep Kosongo distracted. Don't worry, we'll be back soon."

"Those kids are nuts," commented Joel.

"No, it's their normal state. What can we do?" the grandmother moaned.

"Don't tell us to pray, Brother Fernando!" Angie exclaimed. "There must be something more practical we can do."

"I don't know what you're going to do, miss. As for me, I feel confident that the young pair will be back. In the meantime, I have to find out about my fellow missionaries," he informed them, getting to his feet and shaking the cockroaches off his trousers.

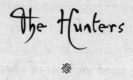
The Hunters

ALEXANDER AND NADIA WANDERED THROUGH the trees with no idea of where they were going. Alexander found a leech clinging to his leg, swollen with his blood, and pulled it off without a fuss. He had encountered leeches in the Amazon and wasn't afraid of them, though they still turned his stomach. There was no way they could get their bearings in the wild jungle growth; everything looked the same. The only spots of color in the eternal green of the forest were the orchids and the fleeting, gaily colored birds. They were walking over soft, reddish dirt, rain-soaked and strewn with obstacles, where at any moment they might take a false step. Treacherous swamps lay hidden beneath mantles of floating leaves. They had to pull aside the vines that grew as solid as curtains, and avoid the piercing thorns of some plants. Even so, the forest was not as impenetrable as it had seemed before; there were occasional openings among the treetops that allowed rays of sun to filter through.

Alexander had his knife in his hand, ready to stab

the first edible animal he could catch, but none gave him that satisfaction. Several rats scurried between his legs, but they were too quick. The two had to stave off their hunger with some bitter, unidentifiable fruit. Since Boroba was eating them, they assumed they weren't harmful and followed his lead. They were afraid of getting lost—which in fact they already were; they hadn't a clue how to get back to Ngoubé or how to find the Pygmies. Their one hope was that the Pygmies would find them.

They had been wandering for several hours, increasingly lost and concerned, when Boroba started shrieking. The little monkey had adopted the habit of sitting atop Alexander's head, where he clung to the young man's ears and coiled his tail around his neck; from that vantage he could see more of the world than in Nadia's arms. Alexander would shake him off, but given the slightest opening Boroba would leap back to his favorite perch. Because he was high on Alexander's head, it was he who saw the tracks. They were only three feet away but were nearly invisible, the tracks of huge feet that flattened everything in their path, leaving a discernible trail. The young people recognized them immediately from having seen them on Michael Mushaha's safari.

"Those are elephant tracks," said Alexander, encouraged. "If there's an elephant anywhere near, the Pygmies will be close by."

The elephant had been pursued for days. The Pygmies' method was to trail their prey, wearing it down completely, then herd it toward their nets and corner it; that was when they attacked. The only break this animal had had was when Beyé-Dokou and his companions were diverted while leading the foreigners to the village of Ngoubé. During that afternoon and part of the night, the elephant had tried to get back to its own territory, but it was fatigued and confused. The hunters had forced it into unfamiliar terrain; it couldn't find its way and was wandering in circles. The presence of the humans with their spears and nets signaled the end; instinct told it that, but it kept running because it was not ready to die.

Over thousands and thousands of years, the elephant has confronted the hunter. In the genetic memories of both is inscribed the tragic ceremony of the hunt, in which each is prepared to kill or to die. The vertigo of danger is mesmerizing for both. At the culminating moment of the hunt, nature holds its breath, the forest falls silent, the breeze becomes still, and at the end, when the fate of one, or of both, is decided, the hearts of man and beast beat in one rhythm. The elephant is the king of the jungle, its largest and heaviest beast, the most respected; no other animal opposes it. Its one enemy is man, a small, vulnerable creature without claws or fangs that with one foot it can crush like a lizard. How does that insignificant being dare claim supremacy? But once the ritual of the hunt is begun, there is no time to contemplate the irony of the situation: Hunter and prey know that the dance can end only in death.

The Pygmy hunters had discovered the trail of flattened vegetation and ripped out tree branches long before Nadia and Alexander made their discovery. They had been following the elephant for hours, moving in perfect coordination to surround it from a prudent distance. This was an aged and solitary male, gifted with two enormous tusks. They were only a dozen Pygmies, with primitive weapons, but they were not going to let it escape. In former times the women had been the ones to tire the animal and drive it toward the traps where the men were waiting.

Years earlier, in the days of their freedom, the Pygmies always had ceremonies to invoke the aid of their ancestors and to thank the animal for submitting to death, but since Kosongo had imposed his reign of terror, nothing had been the same. Even the hunt, the oldest and most fundamental activity of the tribe, had lost its sacred meaning to become nothing but a slaughter.

Alexander and Nadia had heard loud trumpeting and felt the thundering of enormous feet on the ground. But now the final act had begun; the nets had immobilized the elephant and the first spears had been driven into its side.

Nadia's cry stopped the hunters with spears uplifted as the elephant thrashed about furiously, fighting with its last forces.

"Don't kill it! Don't kill it!" Nadia screamed.

The girl stepped between the men and the animal, holding her arms high. The Pygmies rapidly recovered from their surprise and tried to push her aside, but by then Alexander had taken over.

"Enough! Stop! Don't do that!" he yelled, waving the amulet before their eyes.

"Ipemba-Afua!" they exclaimed, falling to the ground before the sacred symbol of their tribe, which had been in Kosongo's hands for so long.

Alexander realized that the carved bone was more

valuable than the powder it contained; even had it been empty, the Pygmies' reaction would have been the same. That object had passed down through many generations, and to them it had magical powers. The debt they owed Alexander and Nadia for having returned Ipemba-Afua was enormous; they could not deny anything to the young foreigners who had brought back the soul of their tribe.

Before he handed them the amulet, Alexander outlined the reasons for not killing the animal they had already trapped in their nets.

"There are very few elephants in the jungle; soon there will be none. What will you do then? There won't be any ivory to buy your children out of slavery. The solution isn't more ivory; the solution is to eliminate Kosongo and free your families once and for all."

He added that Kosongo was an ordinary man, that the earth didn't tremble when his feet touched it, that he could not kill with his gaze or his voice. The only power he had was the power others gave him. If no one was afraid of him, Kosongo would be reduced to normal size.

"And Mbembelé? And the soldiers?" the Pygmies asked.

Alexander had to admit that he hadn't seen the

commandant, and that it was true that the men of the Brotherhood of the Leopard seemed dangerous.

"But if you are brave enough to hunt elephants with spears, you can defy Mbembelé and his men," he added.

"Let's go to the village. With Ipemba-Afua and our women, we can defeat the king and the commandant," Beyé-Dokou proposed.

In his role as *tuma*—greatest hunter—Beyé-Dokou could count on the respect of his companions, but he didn't have the authority to force them to do anything. The hunters began arguing among themselves, but as serious as the subject was, they still burst out laughing from time to time. Alexander felt that his new friends were losing precious time.

"We will liberate your women so they can fight alongside us. My friends will help, too. I'm sure my grandmother will think of something; she's very clever," Alexander promised.

Beyé-Dokou translated his words but was not able to convince the other Pygmies. They believed that this pathetic handful of foreigners would not be very helpful when the moment came to fight. They had not been impressed by the grandmother; she was just an old woman with spiked hair and crazy eyes. As for them, they could be counted on the fingers of two hands, and they had no weapons but spears and nets, while their enemies were numerous and very powerful.

"The women told me that during the reign of Queen Nana-Asante, the Pygmies and the Bantus were friends," Nadia reminded them.

"That's true," said Beyé-Dokou.

"The Bantus in Ngoubé are terrorized as well. Mbembelé tortures them and kills them if they disobey. They would do anything to be free of Kosongo and the commandant. Maybe they'll come over to our side," the girl suggested.

"Even if the Bantus help us and we defeat the soldiers, there's still Sombe, the sorcerer," Beyé-Dokou argued.

"We can beat him, too!" Alexander exclaimed.

But the hunters emphatically rejected the idea of challenging Sombe and listed some of his awesome powers: He swallowed fire; he walked on air and over glowing coals, he could turn into a toad; and his saliva was lethal. They got tangled in the limitations of mime, and all Alexander could make of that was that the wizard would get down on all fours and vomit, which didn't seem to have much connection with the powers of the other world.

"Don't worry, friends, we'll take care of Sombe," Alex promised, with an excess of confidence.

He handed them the magic amulet, which the Pygmies received with emotion and joy. They had awaited this moment for years.

While Alexander was discussing tactics with the Pygmies, Nadia had gone over to the wounded elephant and was trying to calm it, using the language she'd learned from Kobi, the safari elephant. The enormous beast was at the limit of its strength: It was bleeding from the ribs, where two of the hunters' spears had pierced the flesh, and from its trunk, which it was pounding against the ground. The voice of the girl speaking in the elephant's tongue came from very far away, as if in a dream. It was the first time the elephant had confronted humans, and it hadn't expected them to speak as they did. It listened, finally, from pure fatigue. Slowly, but surely, the sound of that voice penetrated the dense barriers of desperation, pain, and terror and reached its brain. Gradually it grew calmer and stopped thrashing about in the nets. Soon it was standing quietly, sides heaving, its eyes fixed on Nadia and fanning its large ears. The smell of fear was so strong that it hit Nadia like a blow, but she kept on talking, sure now that the beast was understanding her. To the Pygmies' astonishment, the elephant began to answer, and soon there was no doubt that the girl and the animal were communicating.

"Let's make a deal," Nadia proposed to the hunters. "In exchange for Ipemba-Afua, you will give the elephant back its life."

The amulet meant much more to the Pygmies than the elephant's ivory, but they didn't know how to remove the nets without being crushed by its feet or impaled upon the very tusks they had meant to take to Kosongo. Nadia assured them that they could do it without being harmed. In the meantime, Alexander had moved near enough to examine the slashes in the animal's thick skin.

"It's lost a lot of blood, it's dehydrated, and these wounds may become infected. I'm afraid it's facing a slow, painful death," he pronounced.

At that point Beyé-Dokou came over to the beast, amulet in hand. He removed a small stopper in one end of Ipemba-Afua; he tipped the bone and shook it like a salt shaker, while another of the hunters cupped his hands to catch the greenish powder that spilled out. They gestured to Nadia that she should apply it; neither of them dared touch the elephant. Nadia explained to the beast that she was going to heal its wounds, and when she saw it had understood, she sprinkled the powder onto the deep cuts from the spears.

The wounds did not close magically, as she had hoped, but within a few minutes the bleeding ceased. The elephant turned its head to feel along its side with its trunk, but Nadia warned it not to touch the injuries.

The Pygmies worked up their courage and removed the nets, a task considerably more complicated than the act of dropping them, but eventually the aged elephant was free. It had resigned itself to its fate, perhaps it had even crossed the frontier between life and death, only to find itself suddenly, miraculously, freed. It took a few tentative steps, then staggered off into the thicket. At the last moment, before it disappeared into the jungle, it turned toward Nadia and, looking at her through one incredulous eye, lifted its trunk and trumpeted.

"What did it say?" Alexander asked.

"If we need help, call," Nadia translated.

Soon it would be night. Nadia had eaten very little in recent days, and Alexander was as starved as she was. The hunters found the tracks of a buffalo but didn't follow them, because those animals were dangerous and moved in a herd. Their tongues were as rough as sandpaper: They could peel off a man's flesh by licking him, they said, and leave nothing but bones. They couldn't hunt buffalo without the aid of their women. At a trot, the Pygmies led Alexander and Nadia to a group of tiny huts made of branches and leaves. It was such a miserable little settlement that it didn't seem possible that humans could live there. They hadn't built anything sturdier because they were nomadic, they were separated from their families, and now they had to travel farther and farther in their search for elephants. The tribe owned nothing, only what each individual could carry. The Pygmies fashioned the basic articles for surviving in the forest and for the hunt; everything else they obtained through trading. Since they weren't interested in civilization, other tribes thought they were very primitive.

From near the huts, the hunters unearthed half an antelope, thickly coated with dirt and insects. They had killed it a couple of days before, and after eating part of it had buried the rest to prevent animals from dragging it off. When they found it was still there, they began singing and dancing. Nadia and Alexander learned once more that despite their travails, the Pygmies were happy when they were in the forest; any pretext was an excuse to joke, tell stories, and laugh uproariously.

The meat smelled ripe and was greenish in color, but thanks to Alexander's cigarette lighter and the Pygmies' skill in scouting out dry tinder, they built a small fire and roasted the meat. The natives also enthusiastically ate the larvae, caterpillars, worms, and ants cooked along with the meat, true delicacies in their minds, and they all topped off the meal with wild fruit, nuts, and water from nearby puddles.

"My grandmother warned us that unpurified water would give us cholera," said Alexander as he gulped from his cupped hands; he was dying of thirst.

"You, maybe, you're so delicate," Nadia teased him. "But I grew up in the Amazon; I'm immune to tropical diseases."

They asked Beyé-Dokou how far it was to Ngoubé, but he couldn't give them a precise answer; for his people, distance was measured in hours and by how quickly they traveled. Five hours walking was equivalent to two running. Neither could he point out the direction, because they had never used a compass or a map and didn't know the four cardinal points. The hunters oriented themselves by the surrounding nature; they could recognize each tree in an area of hundreds of acres. Beyé-Dokou explained that the Pygmies had names for all the trees, plants, and animals; everyone else believed that that the forest was one huge green, swampy morass. The soldiers and the Bantus ventured only between the village and the fork of the river, the place where they maintained contact with the outside world and negotiated with smugglers.

"Traffic in ivory is prohibited in almost every part of the world. How do they get it out of the region?" asked Alexander.

Beyé-Dokou informed him that Mbembelé bribed the authorities and counted on the help of a network of cronies along the river. They tied the tusks underneath the boats, and because the contraband was underwater, there was no difficulty transporting it in broad daylight. Diamonds left in the stomachs of the smugglers. They swallowed them with spoonfuls of honey and cassava pudding, and a couple of days later, when they were in a safe place, eliminated them, a rather revolting procedure, but safe.

The hunters told them about the old days before Kosongo, when Nana-Asante had reigned in Ngoubé. In that time there was no gold and no traffic in ivory. The Bantus earned a livelihood from coffee, which they took downriver to sell in the cities, and the Pygmies stayed most of the year in the forest, hunting.

The Bantus cultivated vegetables and cassava, which they traded to the Pygmies for meat. They celebrated the same festivals. They shared the same poverty, but at least they were free. Sometimes boats came bringing things from the city, but the Bantus bought very little—they were too poor—and the Pygmies weren't interested. The government had forgotten them, although from time to time they sent a nurse with vaccines, or a teacher with the idea of starting a school, or an official who promised to install electricity. They soon left; they couldn't live that far from civilization. They got sick; they went mad. The only ones who had stayed were Commandant Mbembelé and his men.

"And the missionaries?" Nadia asked.

"They were strong, and they stayed, too. But by the time they came, Nana-Asante was already gone. Mbembelé ordered them out, but they didn't leave. They tried to help our tribe. Then they disappeared," the hunters reported.

"Like the queen," Alexander noted.

"No, not like the queen . . ." they replied, but they didn't want to explain any further.

CHAPTER TEN

The Village of the Ancestors

❖

FOR NADIA AND ALEXANDER, IT was a very long night in the forest. The night before they had been at Kosongo's celebration, then Nadia had visited the Pygmy slave women, stolen the amulet, and set fire to the royal hut before leaving the village, so the night hadn't seemed long. This one seemed eternal. Beneath the treetops light faded early and returned late. For more than ten hours, they were huddled together in the hunters' pathetic shelters, enduring dampness, insects, and the proximity of wild animals—none of which disturbed the Pygmies, who feared nothing but ghosts.

The first light of dawn found Nadia, Alexander, and Borobá awake and hungry. Nothing remained of the roasted antelope but burned bones, and they didn't dare eat more fruit because it had given them stomach cramps. They were determined not to think about food. Soon the Pygmies were awake, too, and they talked among themselves in their language for a long time. Since they didn't have a chief, decisions required hours of discussion spent sitting in a circle, but once they reached an agreement, they acted as one. Thanks to her amazing gift for languages, Nadia captured the general sense of the conference. Alexander, on the other hand, caught only a few names: Ngoubé, Ipemba-Afua, Nana-Asante. Finally the animated discussion ended, and the young people were informed of the plan.

The smugglers would be coming to get the ivory—or the Pygmies' children—in a couple of days. That meant they would have to attack Ngoubé within a time frame of thirty-six hours. First, and most important, they decided, was to hold a ceremony with the sacred amulet and ask for the protection of their ancestors and of *Ezenji*, the great spirit of the forest, life, and death.

"Will we be anywhere near the village of the ancestors when we go to Ngoubé?" Nadia asked.

Beyé-Dokou confirmed that in fact the ancestors lived in a place between the river and Ngoubé. It was several hours' travel from where they were at the moment. Alexander remembered that when his grandmother Kate was a young woman backpacking around the world, she often slept in cemeteries because they were so safe; no one came there at night. The village of the ghosts was the perfect place to prepare for their attack on Ngoubé. They would be a short distance from their objective and completely safe; Mbembelé and his soldiers would never come near the place.

"This is a very special moment, the most important moment in the history of your tribe. I think you should hold the ceremony in the village of the ancestors," Alexander suggested.

The hunters were dumbfounded at the total ignorance of the young foreigner, and asked if perhaps in his country they had no respect for their ancestors. Alexander had to admit that in the United States ancestors occupied an insignificant place in the social scale. The Pygmies explained that the home of the spirits was a forbidden place; no human could enter there without perishing immediately. They went only to take their dead. When someone in the tribe died, a ceremony was held that lasted one day and one night. Then the eldest women wrapped the corpse in rags and leaves, bound it with rope made of bark fibers—the same they used for their nets—and carried the dead to rest with the ancestors. They approached the village with all haste, deposited their burden, and ran away as quickly as they could. This was always done in the morning, in the full light of day, after many sacrifices. Morning was the only safe time, since the ghosts slept

during the day and came to life by night. If the ancestors were treated with the proper respect, they never
bothered humans, but when they were offended they
were unforgiving. The spirits were feared more than
the gods. They were closer.

Angie Ninderera had told Nadia and Alexander that
in Africa there is a permanent relationship between
human beings and the spiritual world.

"African gods are more compassionate and reason-
able than the gods of other peoples," she had told
them. "They do not punish like the Christian god.
They do not have a hell where souls suffer for all eternity. The worst thing that can happen to an African
soul is to be lost and alone, forever roaming. An
African god would never send his only son to die on a
cross in order to redeem the human sins he can erase
with a single gesture. African gods did not create
humans in their image, nor do they love them, but at
least they leave people in peace. The spirits, in contrast,
are more dangerous because they have the same defects
people have: They're greedy, cruel, and jealous. They
have to be brought gifts to be kept happy. Fortunately
they don't ask for much: a splash of liquor, a cigarette,
the blood of a rooster."

The Pygmies believed they had greatly offended

their ancestors, and that's why they were suffering at the hands of Kosongo. They didn't know what their offense was, or how to mend it, but they believed that their luck would change if they soothed the ancestors' anger.

"Let's go to their village and ask them why they are offended, and what they want of you," Alexander proposed.

"They're *ghosts!*" the Pygmies exclaimed, horrified.

"Nadia and I aren't afraid of them. We will go talk with them; maybe they will help us. After all, you are their descendants; they must feel a little sympathy for you."

At first the idea was rejected out of hand, but the two foreigners insisted and, after debating a long while, the hunters agreed to go as far as the outskirts of the forbidden village. They would stay concealed in the forest, where they would be preparing their weapons and holding a ceremony while the foreigners attempted to talk with the ancestors.

They walked for hours through the forest. Nadia and Alexander let themselves be led without asking any questions, although sometimes it seemed to them that they had passed the same place several times. The hunters moved forward confidently, always at a trot, without eating or drinking, impervious to fatigue, sustained only by the black tobacco in their bamboo pipes. Except for nets, spears, and darts, those pipes were their only earthly possessions. Alexander and Nadia followed along, stumbling and tripping, dizzy from exhaustion and the heat, until they simply sat down on the ground, refusing to go any farther. They had to rest and eat something.

One of the hunters shot a dart at a monkey, which fell like a stone at their feet. They cut it into pieces, skinned it, and sank their teeth into the raw flesh. Alexander lighted a small fire and roasted the pieces he and Nadia ate, while Borobá covered his face with his hands and moaned. To him it was a revolting act of cannibalism. Nadia offered him bamboo shoots and tried to explain that given the circumstances they could not refuse the meat. Borobá, however, unnerved, turned his back and would not let her touch him.

"How would you feel if a group of monkeys were eating a human in front of us," Nadia said.

"I realize that we're doing something really awful, Eagle, but if we don't have food, we can't go on," Alexander argued.

Beyé-Dokou explained what the Pygmies planned

to do. They would go into Ngoubé at dusk the next day, when Kosongo was expecting his quota of ivory. He would, predictably, be furious when he saw them coming with empty hands. While some of them distracted him with excuses and promises, others would bring weapons and would open the pen where the women were kept. They were going to fight for their lives and rescue their children, they said.

"That sounds like a very brave decision, but not a very practical one," Nadia protested. "It will end in a massacre, because the soldiers have rifles."

"They're ancient," Alexander reminded her.

"Yes, but they still kill from a distance. You can't fight firearms with spears," Nadia insisted.

"Then we have to get control of the ammunition."

"Impossible. The weapons are always loaded and the soldiers wear cartridge belts. Is there some way we can disable the rifles?"

"I don't know anything about those things, Eagle, but my grandmother has reported several wars and lived for months with guerrillas in Central America. I'm sure that she'll know how to do it. We'll have to go back to Ngoubé and set things up before the Pygmies come in."

"How will we do that without the soldiers seeing us?" Nadia asked.

"We'll go in at night. It's my impression that the distance between Ngoubé and the village of the ancestors is relatively short."

"Why is it you're so set on going to that forbidden village, Jaguar?"

"They say that faith moves mountains, Eagle. If we can convince the Pygmies that their ancestors are protecting them, they will feel invincible. And they also have Ipemba-Afua; that will make them even braver."

"And what if the ancestors don't want to help?"

"There *are* no ancestors, Eagle. The village is nothing but a cemetery. We can spend a few quiet hours there, then go and tell our new friends that the ancestors promised support in the battle against Mbembelé. That's my plan."

"I don't like your plan. When you're not honest, things never turn out right," said Nadia.

"If you want, I can go alone."

"You know that we're supposed to stay together. I'll go with you," she decided.

There was still light when they reached the place where they had earlier seen the bloody voodoo dolls. The Pygmies refused to go any farther; they could not take one step into the domain of the hungry spirits.

"I don't believe that ghosts get hungry. How could they if they don't have a stomach?" Alexander commented.

Beyé-Dokou pointed to the mounds of garbage scattered everywhere. His tribe made sacrifices of animals and brought offerings of fruit, honey, nuts, and liquor to lay at the feet of the dolls. At night most of it disappeared, swallowed up by the insatiable specters. Because of the offerings they lived in peace; if the spirits were fed as they were supposed to be, they didn't attack human beings. Alex hinted that rats must have eaten the food that was left, but the Pygmies were offended and flatly rejected that theory. The elderly women who were responsible for taking the bodies to the entrance of the village of the spirits after the funeral rituals could testify that they saw food there. Sometimes they heard horrifying yells that reached such heights of terror that they turned the mourner's hair white within hours.

"Nadia, Borobá, and I will go, but we need someone to wait for us here and take us on to Ngoubé before daylight," said Alexander.

For the Pygmies, the fact that the two young foreigners were going to spend the night in the cemetery was absolute proof that they were not right in the head, but since they couldn't dissuade them, they accepted their decision. Beyé-Dokou pointed out the direction they should take, told them good-bye with great outpourings of affection and sadness—because he was sure he would never see them again—but out of courtesy agreed to wait for them at the voodoo altar till sunup. The other Pygmies also bid them farewell, awed by the bravery of their young friends.

Nadia and Alexander were interested to find that in this voracious jungle, where only elephants left visible tracks, there was a path leading to the cemetery. That meant that someone was using it frequently.

"The ancestors pass this way," murmured Nadia.

"If they did exist, Eagle, they wouldn't leave footprints and they wouldn't need a path," Alexander replied.

"How do you know that?"

"It's a question of logic."

"There is nothing in this world that would get either the Pygmies or the Bantus near this place, and Mbembelé's soldiers are even more superstitious; they won't come into the forest at all. So tell me, who made this path?" she demanded.

"I don't know, but we're going to find out."

After a half hour of walking, they suddenly emerged into a clearing among the trees. Before them was a high, thick circular wall constructed of stones, logs, straw, and clay. Hanging on the wall were skulls and bones, the dried heads of animals, masks, carved wood figures, clay pots, and amulets. There was no visible door, but they discovered a round opening almost three feet wide located some distance above the ground.

"I'll bet the old women who bring the corpses here push them through that hole. There must be piles of bones on the other side," said Alexander.

Nadia wasn't tall enough to see, but Alex looked inside.

"What's in there?" she asked.

"I can't see very well. Let's send Borobá in to check it out."

"Not on your life! Borobá's not going in there alone. We all go or no one goes," Nadia said decisively.

"Wait here; I'll be right back," Alexander answered.

"I'd rather go with you."

Alexander speculated that if he crawled through the hole, he would fall on his head. He didn't know what to expect on the other side; it made more sense to go over the wall—child's play for him given his experience in mountain climbing. The irregular surface made the climb easy, and in less than two minutes he was straddling the wall, while Nadia and Borobá waited nervously below.

"It's like an abandoned village. It looks very old. I've never seen anything like it," said Alexander.

"Do you see skeletons?" Nadia asked.

"No. Everything is clean and bare. Maybe they don't put the bodies through that hole, as we thought . . ."

With her friend's help, Nadia also climbed over the wall. Borobá hesitated, but the fear of being left alone galvanized him, so he followed; he was never far from his mistress.

At first inspection the village of the ancestors seemed to be a collection of clay and stone ovens arranged in concentric circles, in perfect symmetry. In each of those round constructions was a hole that served as a door of sorts, covered with lengths of cloth or tree bark. There were no statues, dolls, or amulets. All life seemed to have stopped in the area inside the high wall. There was no hint of jungle growth, and even the temperature was different. An inexplicable silence reigned; the hubbub of monkeys and birds was absent, as was the drumming of rain or murmur of the breeze in the leaves. The silence was total.

"These are tombs; they must bury the dead in them.

Let's look inside," Alexander proposed.

When they lifted some of the curtains veiling the openings, they saw pyramidal piles of human remains. The skeletons were dry and brittle, and perhaps some had been there for hundreds of years. A number of the huts were filled with bones; others were half filled, while some were entirely empty.

"What an eerie sight!" Alexander observed with a shiver.

"I don't understand, Jaguar. If no one comes here, how can everything be so orderly and clean?" asked Nadia.

"It's very mysterious," her friend agreed.

CHAPTER ELEVEN

Encounter with the Spirits

❖

THE LIGHT, WHICH WAS ALWAYS faint beneath the green canopy of the jungle, was beginning to fade. For a couple of days—from the time they left Ngoubé—the friends had seen the sky only through occasional open spaces among the treetops. The cemetery was in a clearing, and overhead they could see a patch of sky starting to turn dark blue. They sat down between two tombs, prepared to spend a few hours in solitude.

In the three years that had passed since Alexander and Nadia had met, their friendship had grown like a great tree, until it had become the most important thing in their lives. The youthful friendship of the first months had evolved as they matured, though they never spoke of it. They lacked words to describe that delicate sentiment, and feared that if they talked about it, it would shatter like glass. To express their relationship in words would be to define it, put limits on it, diminish it. As long as they never spoke of it, it would remain open, and uncontaminated. So the friendship had quietly expanded in silence, without their having noticed.

Recently Alexander had experienced more rudely than ever the hormonal explosions of adolescence that most teenagers suffer at an earlier age. His body was his enemy; it would not leave him in peace. His grades at school had dropped, he wasn't keeping up with his music, and even the climbing excursions with his father to the mountains, which had been such a basic part of his life, now bored him. He suffered fits of melancholy and fought with his family, and later, remorseful, didn't know how to make peace. He did everything clumsily, tangled in a morass of conflicting emotions. He moved from depression to euphoria in a matter of minutes; his feelings were so intense that at times he seriously asked himself whether it was worth the pain to go on living. In moments of deepest pessimism he believed that the world was a disaster and that the greater part of humanity was hopelessly stupid. Although he had read books about adolescence, and it had been thoroughly discussed in school, he was suffering as if he had an incurable illness. "Don't worry, we've all gone through the same thing," his father consoled him, as if he had no more than a cold. But Alexander was eighteen, and he wasn't getting any better. He could barely communicate with his parents; at times they drove him crazy. He thought of them as being from another era; everything they said sounded out of date. He knew that they loved him unconditionally, and he was grateful to them for that, but he was convinced that they couldn't possibly understand him.

The only person he could share his problems with was Nadia. In the coded language he used in his e-mails, he could describe the things happening to him and not feel embarrassed, something he wasn't able to do in person. She accepted him as he was and never judged him. She read his messages without offering an opinion, because in truth she didn't know what to answer; her worries were different ones.

Alexander felt that his obsession with girls was ridiculous, but he couldn't help it. A word, a gesture, brushing past a girl, was all it took to fill his head with images and his heart with desire. The best treatment was exercise: He surfed winter and summer in the Pacific. The shock of the icy water and the marvelous sensation of skimming over the waves brought back the innocence and euphoria of childhood, though that state of mind did not last very long. The trips with his grandmother, on the other hand, kept him distracted for weeks. He was able to control his emotions in front of her, and that gave him a little hope. Maybe his father was right, and this madness would not last forever.

Ever since they had met in New York at the beginning of this trip, Alexander had looked at Nadia through new eyes, although he excluded her completely from his romantic fantasies. He couldn't imagine her in that light; he thought of her in the same way he thought of his sisters, with a pure and possessive affection. His role was to protect Nadia from anyone who might do her harm, especially other males. Nadia was pretty—at least he thought so—and sooner or later there would be a swarm of guys hitting on her. He would never allow all those drones to get near her; the mere idea made him frantic. He was aware of Nadia's body, the grace of her movements, and the concentration of her expression. He liked her coloring: the dark blond hair, the toasty skin, the eyes golden as hazelnuts. An artist could paint her portrait with a minimal palette of yellow and chestnut. She was different from him, and that intrigued him: her physical fragility, which hid great strength of character, her quiet way of listening, the way she harmonized with nature. She had always been reserved, but now she seemed mysterious. He was enchanted to be near her, to touch her occasionally, but it was much easier to communicate with her from a distance. When they were together, he bumbled and stumbled; he didn't know what to say to her and had begun to weigh his words. It seemed that sometimes his hands were too heavy, his feet too big, his voice too domineering.

Sitting there in the darkness, surrounded by the tombs in a centuries-old Pygmy cemetery, Alexander felt the nearness of his friend with painful intensity. He loved her more than anyone in the world, more than his parents and all his friends put together. He was afraid of losing her.

"Tell me more about how you like New York. Are you enjoying living with my grandmother?" he asked, just to start a conversation.

"Your grandmother treats me like a princess, but I miss my father."

"Don't go back to the Amazon, Eagle. It's too far away; we can't keep in touch."

"Come with me," she said.

"I'll go wherever you want, but first I have to get through med school."

"Your grandmother says that you're writing about our adventures in the Amazon and in the Kingdom of the Golden Dragon. Will you also be writing about the Pygmies?" Nadia asked.

"It's just notes, Eagle. I don't pretend to be a writer; I'm going to be a doctor. I got the idea when my mother was ill, and I made up my mind that time in the Himalayas when I watched Tensing heal your shoulder with needles and prayers. I realized that science and technology aren't enough to make someone well; there are other, equally important, factors. Holistic medicine. That's what I want to do," Alexander explained.

"Don't you remember what the shaman Walimai told you? He said that you have the power to cure people, and that you should use that gift. I think you will make the best doctor in the world," Nadia assured him.

"And what about you? What do you want to do when you finish school?"

"I'm going to study the language of animals."

Alexander laughed. "There isn't any institution for that."

"Then I'll start the first one."

"It would work out well for us to travel together. Me as a doctor and you as a linguist," Alexander proposed.

"That will be when we're married," Nadia replied.

The sentence lingered on the air, visible as a flag. Alexander felt his blood racing like an army of ants in his veins, and his heart was pounding out of his chest. He was so surprised he couldn't answer. Why hadn't he thought of that? He'd always been "in love" with Cecilia Burns, but he had nothing in common with her. This last year he had stubbornly pursued her, stoically accepting her moods and whims. While he was still behaving like a kid, Cecilia Burns had turned into a full-blown woman, even though they were almost the same age. She was very attractive, and Alexander had lost any hope of her ever noticing him. Cecilia wanted to be an actress; she swooned over movie stars and planned to test her luck in Hollywood the minute she turned eighteen. Nadia's comment unveiled a horizon that he had never considered until that moment.

"What an idiot I am!" he blurted out.

"What do you mean by that? That we're not going to marry?"

"I . . ." Alexander mumbled.

"Look, Jaguar. We don't know whether we'll ever get out of this jungle alive. Since we don't have much time, let's speak with our hearts," she proposed earnestly.

"Of course we'll get married, Eagle! No question about it," he replied, with his ears blazing.

"All right, then," she said, shrugging her shoulders. "We have a few years before that happens."

For a long time, they had nothing more to say. Alexander was shaken by a hurricane of conflicting ideas and emotions, which ranged from the anxiety of looking Nadia in the eye in broad daylight to the temptation to grab her and kiss her. He was sure that he would never dare do that. The silence was unbearable.

"Are you afraid, Jaguar?" Nadia asked a half hour later.

Alexander didn't answer, thinking that she had read his mind and was referring to the new fear she had awakened in him, the thoughts that were paralyzing him that very minute. With her second question, he understood that she was talking about something much more immediate and concrete.

"Tomorrow we have to face Kosongo, Mbembelé, and maybe the witch man Sombe. How do we do that?"

"It will work out, Eagle. As my grandmother says, you must never fear fear."

Alexander was grateful she had changed the subject, and decided that he wouldn't speak of love again, at least not until he was safe in California, separated from her by the breadth of the continent. It would be a little easier to talk about emotions by e-mail, when she couldn't see his red ears.

"I hope that the eagle and the jaguar will come to our aid," said Alexander.

"We'll need more than that this time," Nadia concluded.

They were interrupted by the sense of a silent presence that had appeared as if answering a call. Alexander grabbed his knife and switched on the flashlight. The beam of light revealed a terrifying figure.

Immobilized by shock, they saw, no farther than ten feet from them, a witchlike form wrapped in tattered rags. The skeleton-thin body was topped with a great mane of tangled white hair. Their first thought was that it was a ghost, but Alexander immediately reasoned that there had to be another explanation.

"Who's there!" he shouted in English, jumping to his feet.

Silence. He repeated the question and again focused the flashlight on the figure.

"Are you a spirit?" Nadia asked in a mixture of French and Bantu.

The apparition answered with an incomprehensible murmur and backed away, blinded by the light.

"I think it's an old woman!" Nadia exclaimed.

And then they understood what the supposed ghost was saying: Nana-Asante.

"Nana-Asante? The queen of Ngoubé? Are you alive or dead?" Nadia asked.

They quickly learned the truth. *This* was the former queen in the flesh, the woman who had disappeared, apparently murdered by Kosongo when he usurped the throne. The woman had hidden for years in the cemetery, living off the offerings the hunters left for the ancestors. She was the one who had kept the place clean; she entombed the corpses pushed through the opening in the wall.

She told Alex and Nadia that she wasn't alone but in very good company—the company of the spirits, whom she expected to join soon. She was tired of inhabiting her body. She told them that once she had been a *nganga*, a healer who moved in the world of the spirits after she fell into a trance. She had seen them during ceremonies and had always been afraid of them, but since she had been living in the cemetery she had lost that fear. Now the spirits were her friends.

"Poor woman, she must have gone mad," Alexander whispered to Nadia.

Nana-Asante was not mad. To the contrary, those years of seclusion had given her exceptional lucidity. She was informed about everything that was happening in Ngoubé. She knew about Kosongo and his twenty wives, about Mbembelé and his ten soldiers of the Brotherhood of the Leopard, about the sorcerer Sombe and his demons. She knew that the Bantus of the village hadn't dared stand up to them because they inflicted horrible torture at the least sign of rebellion. She knew that the Pygmies had become slaves, that Kosongo had taken their sacred amulet, and that Mbembelé sold their children if they did not bring him ivory. And she knew, too, that just recently a group of foreigners had come to Ngoubé looking for the missionaries, and that the two youngest had escaped from Ngoubé and would come to visit her. She had been waiting for them.

"How could you know that!" Alexander burst out.

"The ancestors told me. They know many things. They do not go out only at night, as people believe. They also go out during the day; they walk with other spirits of nature, here and there, among the living and the dead. They know that you will come to them to ask for help," said Nana-Asante.

"And will they agree to help their descendants?" asked Nadia.

"I don't know. You will have to speak with them."

An enormous full moon, yellow and radiant, rose over the clearing in the jungle. While it was shining, something magic happened in the cemetery, something that in years to come Alexander and Nadia would remember as one of the pivotal moments of their lives.

The first sign that something phenomenal was occurring was that Alex and Nadia could see perfectly, as if the cemetery were lighted by enormous stadium lamps. For the first time since they'd been in Africa, they were cold. Shivering, they hugged each other for courage and warmth. A growing murmur, like bees, filled the air, and before the young people's astounded eyes the clearing filled with translucent beings. They were surrounded with spirits. It was impossible to describe them because they had no defined form. They seemed vaguely human, but they changed constantly as if sketched in smoke. They were neither naked nor clothed; they had no color but were luminous.

The intense musical hum of insects vibrating in their ears had meaning; it was a universal language they understood, a kind of telepathy. They had to explain nothing to the spirits, tell them nothing, ask them nothing—in words. Those ethereal beings knew all that had ever happened and all that would take place in the future: Time did not exist in their dimension. There were souls of dead ancestors and of beings yet to be born, souls that remained indefinitely in a spiritual state and others ready to take on physical form on this planet or on others.

The friends learned that the spirits rarely intervene in events of the material world, although sometimes they assist animals through intuition and humans through imagination, dreams, creativity, and mystic or spiritual revelation. Most people live their lives without any link with the divine and do not note the signs, coincidences, premonitions, and small daily miracles in which the supernatural is manifest. Alex and Nadia learned that the spirits do not cause illness, misfortune, or death, as they had heard; suffering is caused by the wickedness and ignorance of the living. Neither do they destroy people who violate or intrude into their domains, because they have no domains and it is not possible to offend them. Sacrifices, gifts, and prayers do not reach them; their only usefulness is to mollify the mourners making the offerings.

The silent dialogue with the ghosts lasted for a time impossible to calculate. Gradually the light grew brighter still, and the space around them opened to a larger dimension. The wall they had climbed to get inside the cemetery dissolved, and they found themselves in the midst of a forest, although it seemed different from where they had been before. Nothing was the same; everything emitted a radiant energy. The trees no longer formed a compact mass of vegetation; now each had its own character, its name, its memories. The tallest among them, from whose seeds other, younger trees had grown, told them their stories. The longest-living plants revealed that imminently they would die and replenish the earth, while the newest stretched out tender shoots to grasp onto life. Nature's continuous murmuring denoted subtle forms of communication among the species.

Hundreds of animals surrounded Alexander and Nadia, some they had never known existed: strange okapis with long necks like small giraffes; musk deer; civet cats; mongooses; flying squirrels; golden cats; and antelopes striped like zebras. There were scaly anteaters and a horde of monkeys in the trees, chattering like children in the magical light of that night. A parade of leopards, crocodiles, rhinoceroses, and other beasts passed before them in perfect harmony. Extraordinary birds flooded the air with their songs and lighted the night with their bold plumage. Thousands of insects danced on the breeze: many-colored butterflies, phosphorescent scarabs, noisy crickets, delicate fireflies. The ground seethed with reptiles: snakes, turtles, and large lizards, descendents of the dinosaurs that observed the two young people through three-lidded eyes.

They were in the heart of the spirit forest, surrounded by thousands and thousands of plant and animal souls. Alexander's and Nadia's minds expanded still further, and they perceived the connections among creatures, a universe interlaced with currents of energy, an exquisite network as fine as silk and as strong as steel. They perceived that nothing exists in isolation; everything that happens, from a thought to a hurricane, is cosmic in effect. They sensed the palpitating, living earth, a great organism generating flora and fauna, mountains, rivers, the wind of the plains, the lava of volcanoes, the eternal snows of the highest mountains. That mother planet, they intuited, is a part of other, greater organisms, and is joined to the myriad of stars in the unbounded firmament.

Alexander and Nadia saw the inevitable cycles of life, death, transformation and rebirth as a marvelous design in which all things occur simultaneously, without past, present or future: *now*, forever been and forever being.

And finally, in the last phase of their fantastic odyssey, they understood that the hosts of earthly souls, along with all things in the universe, are particles of a single spirit, like drops of water in an ocean. One spiritual essence animates all existence. There is no separation among beings, no frontier between life and death.

At no moment during that incredible journey were Nadia and Alexander afraid. At first it seemed to them that they were floating in the nebula of a dream, and they felt a profound calm. As their spiritual pilgrimage expanded their senses and imagination, tranquility gave way to euphoria, uncontainable joy, a sensation of tremendous energy and force.

The moon continued its course across the firmament and disappeared among the treetops. For a few minutes, the luminescence of the ghosts lingered as the buzzing sound and the cold gradually diminished. The two friends awakened from their trance and were once again sitting among the tombs, with Borobá clinging to Nadia's waist. For a while neither spoke, or even moved, prolonging the enchantment. Finally they looked at each other, dazed, doubting what they had lived through, but then before them emerged the figure of Queen Nana-Asante, who confirmed that it had not been a hallucination.

The queen was illuminated from within, resplendent. Nadia and Alexander saw her as she was and not in the guise in which she had at first appeared: a miserable old woman, pure bones and rags. In truth she was formidable, an Amazon, an ancient goddess of the forest. Nana-Asante had grown wise during those years of meditation and solitude among the dead. She had cleansed her heart of hatred and greed; she wanted nothing, she feared nothing . . . nothing disturbed her tranquility. She was brave because she did not cling to life; she was strong because she was motivated by compassion; she was just because she intuited truth; she was invincible because she was supported by a legion of spirits.

"There is great suffering in Ngoubé. During your reign there was peace. The Bantus and the Pygmies remember those times. Come with us, Nana-Asante. Help us," Nadia pleaded.

The queen replied without hesitation, "Let us go." It was as if she had been preparing for this moment for years.

CHAPTER TWELVE

The Reign of Terror

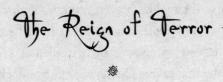

DURING THE TWO DAYS NADIA and Alexander spent in the forest, a series of dramatic events was developing in the village of Ngoubé. Kate, Angie, Brother Fernando, and Joel had not seen Kosongo again and had had to deal with Mbembelé, who by anyone's judgment was much more to be feared than the king. When he learned of the disappearance of two of his prisoners, the commandant had focused more on punishing his guards for having let them get away than on the fate of the missing young people. He made no effort to find them, and when Kate asked for help in searching for them, he refused.

"They're dead by now; I'm not going to waste time on them. No one survives at night in the jungle—except the Pygmies, who aren't human," Mbembelé told her.

"Then send some of the Pygmies with me to look for them," Kate demanded.

It was Mbembelé's custom not to respond to questions, much less requests, with the result that no one dared pose them. The brazen attitude of this foreign woman amazed more than angered him; he couldn't believe he was witnessing such insolence. He stood there without speaking, observing her from behind his sinister mirrored glasses, as sweat ran down his shaved head and the naked arms marked by ritual scars. They were in his "office," where he had had his guards bring the writer.

Mbembelé's office was in the jail, furnished with a pair of chairs and a rickety metal desk in one corner. Horrified, Kate took note of the torture instruments and dark bloodlike stains on the whitewashed clay walls. There was no question that the commandant's purpose in having her brought there was to intimidate her, and he had succeeded, but Kate was determined not to show weakness. She had nothing but an American passport and her journalist's credentials to protect her, but they would be worthless if Mbembelé perceived how frightened she was.

It seemed to her that Mbembelé, unlike King Kosongo, had not swallowed the story that they had come to Ngoubé to interview the king. He undoubtedly suspected that the real cause of their presence there was to discover the fate of the disappeared missionaries. Now they were in Mbembelé's power, but he would have to calculate the risks before he unleashed his cruelty. He couldn't mistreat foreigners, Kate reasoned with excessive optimism. It was one thing to abuse the poor devils he held in his fist in Ngoubé, but something very different to harass white Americans. He did not want to invite an investigation by authorities. The commandant would have to get rid of them as quickly as possible; if they learned too much, he would be left no alternative but to kill them. He knew that they wouldn't leave without Nadia and Alexander, and that complicated things. Kate concluded that they would have to proceed very cautiously, because the commandant's best card would be for his guests to suffer a well-planned accident. It never occurred to Kate that at least one of them was looked upon favorably in Ngoubé.

After a long pause, Mbembelé asked, "What is the name of that other woman in your group?"

"Angie. Angie Ninderera. She flew us here in her plane, but—"

"His Majesty, King Kosongo, is willing to accept her as one of his wives."

Kate felt her knees buckle. Yesterday's joke was now a disagreeable—perhaps dangerous—reality. What would Angie say about having caught Kosongo's eye?

Nadia and Alexander should be showing up soon, according to her grandson's note. On their previous trips, too, she had gone through some desperate moments because of those kids, and both times they had come back safe and sound. She had to trust them. The first thing would be to get the whole group back together; then they would figure out some way to get back to civilization. It occurred to her that the king's sudden interest in Angie could at least help win a little time.

"Do you want me to pass on the king's petition to Angie?" Kate asked when she recovered her voice.

"It isn't a petition; it's an order. Talk with her. I will see her during the tournament. That will be tomorrow. In the meantime, you have permission to move about the village, but I forbid you to go near the royal compound, the Pygmies' corrals, or the well."

The commandant waved a hand, and immediately the soldier at the door seized Kate by the arm and dragged her away. For a moment she was blinded by the light of day.

Kate rejoined her friends and transmitted the declaration of love to Angie, who took it rather badly, as Kate had expected.

"I would never be one of that flock of Kosongo's

women!" she exclaimed, furious.

"Of course you wouldn't, Angie, but you could be nice to him a couple of days and—"

"Not one minute!" Angie sighed. "Of course if it was the commandant, instead of Kosongo—"

"Mbembelé is a beast!" Kate interrupted.

"That's a joke, Kate. I don't intend to be nice to Kosongo, or Mbembelé, or anyone else. I intend to get out of this hole as soon as possible, claim my plane, and get to a place where these criminals can't catch up with me."

"If you distract the king, as Ms. Cold suggests, we can gain some time," Brother Fernando declared.

"How do you suggest I do that? Look at me! My clothes are wet and filthy, I've lost my lipstick, and my hair's a disaster. I look like a porcupine," Angie replied, pointing to dirt-stiffened hair that stuck out in all directions.

"The people in the village are afraid," the missionary interrupted, changing the subject. "No one wants to answer my questions, but I've tied up a few loose ends. I know that my companions were here, and that they disappeared several months ago. They can't have gone anywhere. The most likely answer is that they've become martyrs."

"Does that mean they were killed?" Kate asked.

"Yes. I think they gave their lives for Christ. I pray that at least they didn't suffer long."

"I'm truly sorry, Brother Fernando," Angie said, suddenly serious. "Forgive all my joking and bad humor. You can count on me; I'll do what I can to help you. I'll dance the dance of the seven veils to distract Kosongo, if you want."

"I won't ask that of you, Miss Ninderera," the missionary replied sadly.

"Call me Angie," she said.

They spent the rest of the day waiting for Nadia and Alexander to return, wandering around the village looking for information, and making plans to escape. The two guards who had been careless the night before had been arrested by the soldiers and not replaced, so no one was guarding them. They found out that the soldiers of the Brotherhood of the Leopard, who had deserted from the regular army and come to Ngoubé with the commandant, were the only ones who had access to the firearms kept in the barracks. The Bantu guards were forcibly recruited in their teenage years. They were poorly armed, mainly with machetes and knives, and obeyed more out of fear than from loyalty.

Under orders from the handful of Mbembelé's soldiers, the guards had to contain the rest of the Bantu population, that is, their own families and friends. Fierce discipline left no out; rebels and deserters were executed without a trial.

The women of Ngoubé, who once had been free and involved in the decisions of the community, lost their rights and were forced to work on Kosongo's plantations and look after the needs of the men. The prettiest girls were sent to the king's harem. The commandant's network of spies included children, who were taught to watch their own families. The mere accusation of treachery, whether or not there was proof, was punished by death. In the beginning many were executed, but the population in that area was sparse, and when the king and the commandant saw that they were killing off their subjects, they decided to curb their enthusiasm.

These two leaders also counted on the aid of the witch doctor Sombe, whom they called on when a sorcerer's services were required. People were accustomed to healers or witch men whose mission was to act as liaison with the world of the spirits, cure illness, cast spells, and fashion protective amulets. It was generally believed that a person's death was caused by magic.

When someone died, it was up to the sorcerer to determine who was responsible, then undo the curse and punish the guilty party or force him to pay compensation to the family of the deceased. That gave the healer power in the community. In Ngoubé, as in many other parts of Africa, there had always been sorcerers, some more respected than others, but none as much as Sombe.

No one knew where the bizarre witch doctor lived. He would materialize in the village like a devil, and once he had done what he had come to do, he evaporated without a trace, and no one would see him for weeks or months. He was so feared that even Kosongo and Mbembelé tried to avoid him; both stayed in their quarters when Sombe was due to appear. His appearance alone spread terror. He was enormous—as tall as Commandant Mbembelé—and when he fell into a trance, he acquired supernatural strength; he was able to lift heavy tree trunks that six men couldn't budge. He wore the head of a leopard and a necklace of fingers that—word had it—he had amputated from his victims with the blade of his gaze, just as during his exhibitions of sorcery he decapitated roosters without touching them.

"I would like to meet this famous Sombe," Kate said

when the friends met to report what each of them had found out.

"And I would like to photograph his magic tricks," added Joel.

"Maybe they're not tricks," said Angie, shuddering. "Voodoo magic can be very dangerous."

Their second, seemingly eternal, night in the large hut, the *International Geographic* party kept the torches lit despite the stench of burning resin and clouds of black smoke; at least that way they could see the cockroaches and rats. Kate was awake for hours, listening to every sound, waiting for Nadia and Alexander to show up. Since there were no guards at the open doorway, she could step outside to get a breath when the air in the building became unbearable. Angie joined her outside, and they sat down on the ground, shoulder to shoulder.

"I'm dying for a cigarette," Angie muttered.

"This is your chance to drop the habit. I did. It causes lung cancer," Kate warned her. "Want a swig of vodka?"

"And alcohol's not a vice, Kate." Angie laughed.

"Are you insinuating that I'm an alcoholic? You've got some nerve! I take a few sips from time to time to ease my bones. That's all."

"We have to get out of here, Kate."

"We can't go without my grandson and Nadia," the writer replied.

"How long are you prepared to wait for them? The boats are coming to pick us up day after tomorrow."

"They'll be back by then."

"And if they aren't?"

"In that case all of you can go, but I'm staying," Kate said.

"I won't leave you here alone, Kate."

"You will go with the others to get help. You'll have to get in touch with the people at *International Geographic* and with the American embassy. No one knows where we are."

"Our one hope is that Mushaha picked up one of the messages I sent by radio, but I wouldn't count on that," said Angie.

The two women sat in silence for a long time. Despite the circumstances, they were able to appreciate the beauty of the moonlit night. At that hour there were very few torches lit in the village except for those around the royal compound and the soldiers' barracks. They could hear the never-ceasing sounds of the jungle and smell the penetrating scent of wet earth. A few yards away was a parallel world of creatures that never saw sunlight and that were watching them from the shadows as they talked.

"Do you know what that 'well' is, Angie?" Kate asked.

"The one the missionaries mentioned in their letters?"

"It isn't what we think. It isn't really a well."

"No? What is it then?"

"It's a site of executions."

"What are you saying!" Angie exclaimed.

"Just what I told you, Angie. It's behind the royal compound, enclosed within a palisade. No one can go near it."

"Is it a cemetery, then?"

"No. It's a watering hole, a kind of pond filled with crocodiles."

Angie jumped to her feet, gasping for breath, with the feeling that a locomotive was charging through her breast. Kate's words reaffirmed the terror she had felt ever since her plane crash-landed on the beach and she knew she was trapped in this savage region. Hour by hour, day by day, she became more convinced that she was inescapably heading toward her death. She had always thought she would die in a plane crash until Má Bangesé, the fortune-teller in the market, had told her about the crocodiles. At first she hadn't taken the prophecy too seriously, but after a pair of nearly fatal encounters with the awesome amphibians, the idea had taken root in her mind and become an obsession. Kate guessed what her friend was thinking.

"Don't be superstitious, Angie. The fact that Kosongo keeps crocodiles doesn't mean you're going to be their supper."

"It's my destiny, Kate; I can't escape it."

"We're going to get out of here alive, Angie, I promise."

"You can't promise that because you can't make it happen. What else do you know?"

"They throw anyone who rebels against Kosongo and Mbembelé's authority into that hole," Kate explained. "I learned that from the Pygmy women. Their husbands have to hunt game to feed the crocs. They know everything that goes on in the village. They're slaves of the Bantus, they do all the heavy work, they go into all the huts, they hear all the conversations, they observe. They're locked up only at night—they're free to walk around during the day. No one pays any attention to them because they think they don't have human intelligence."

"Do you think that's how they killed the missionaries, and that's why there's no trace of them?" Angie shivered.

"Yes, but I can't prove it. That's why I haven't told Brother Fernando yet. Tomorrow I'll find out the real truth, and, if possible, I'm going to get a look at that crocodile pool," Kate confided. "We need to photograph it; it's an essential part of the story I'm planning to write for the magazine."

The next day Kate again presented herself before Commandant Mbembelé to tell him that Angie Ninderera felt very honored by the king's attentions and was considering his proposition, but that she needed a few days to decide. She had promised her hand to a very powerful sorcerer in Botswana and, as everyone knew, it was very dangerous to betray a witch doctor, even from a distance.

"In that case King Kosongo is not interested in the woman," the commandant declared.

Kate quickly backpedaled. She hadn't expected Mbembelé to take her that seriously.

"Don't you think you should consult with His Majesty?"

"No."

"Well, Angie didn't exactly give her word to that

man; it's not really a formal engagement, you understand? I've heard that the most powerful sorcerer in Africa—Sombe, isn't it?—lives near here. Maybe he can release Angie from the magic of her other suitor," Kate proposed.

"Maybe."

"When will the famous Sombe be coming to Ngoubé?"

"You ask a lot of questions, old woman. You're as big a pest as the *mopani*," the commandant complained, waving his hand as if brushing away a bee. "I will speak with King Kosongo. We will discuss a way to free the woman."

"One thing more, Commandant Mbembelé," said Kate from the door.

"What do you want now?"

"The building you put us in is very pleasant, but it's a little dirty; there are a lot of rat and bat droppings—"

"And?"

"Angie Ninderera is very delicate. Bad smells make her ill. Could you send us a slave to clean the place and prepare our food? If it isn't too much bother."

"I suppose," the commandant replied.

The servant he assigned them looked like a child. She was wearing a raffia skirt and, though slim and little more than four feet tall, she was very strong. She came equipped with a twig broom and set about sweeping the floor at a furious pace. The more dust she raised, the worse the odor and filth. Kate stopped her, because in fact she had asked for her with other goals in mind: She needed an ally. At first the woman seemed not to understand what Kate wanted. She put on an expression as bland and as blank as a sheep's, but when the writer mentioned Beyé-Dokou, her face lighted up. Kate realized that the stupidity was feigned, purely a defense mechanism.

With mime and a few words in Bantu and French, the Pygmy explained that her name was Jena, and that she was the wife of Beyé-Dokou. They had two children, whom she saw very little of because they were kept in a separate fenced area, but for the moment the children were well cared for by a couple of grandmothers. Tomorrow, however, was the day set for Beyé-Dokou and the other hunters to bring the ivory; if they failed they would lose their children, said Jena, weeping. Kate didn't know how to react to the tears, but Angie and Brother Fernando tried to console Jena with the argument that Kosongo wouldn't dare sell children as long as a group of journalists was around to act as witnesses. Jena was of the opinion that nothing and nobody could change Kosongo's mind.

· · ·

The sinister throbbing of drums filled the African night, reverberating through the jungle and terrorizing the foreigners in their hut, their hearts laden with dark presages.

"What do those drums mean?" asked Joel, trembling.

"I don't know, but it can't be good news," Brother Fernando replied.

"I am *sick* of being afraid all the time!" Angie exclaimed. "I've had a pain in my chest for days from all this anxiety. I can't breathe. I want to get out of here!"

"Let's pray, my friends," the missionary suggested.

A soldier appeared at their door and, speaking directly to Angie, announced that the tournament was about to start and Commandant Mbembelé demanded her presence.

"I will come with my friends," she said.

"However you want," the messenger replied.

"Why are the drums playing?" Angie asked.

"Ezenji," was the soldier's curt reply.

"The dance of death?"

This time he didn't answer, merely turned and left. The members of the group consulted among themselves. Joel was of the opinion that it was their own deaths—that they were slated to be the principals in this spectacle. Kate made him stop.

"You're making me nervous, Joel. If they mean to kill us, they won't do it in public. It's not to their benefit to provoke an international scandal by murdering us."

"Who would ever know, Kate? We're at the mercy of these madmen. What does the opinion of the rest of the world mean to them? They do whatever they please," Joel moaned.

The entire village, except for the Pygmies, had gathered in the plaza. A square had been traced with lime, like a boxing ring, and lit with torches. Beneath the Tree of Words sat the commandant, accompanied by his "officials," that is, the ten soldiers of the Brotherhood of the Leopard, who were standing behind his chair. He was dressed as he always was: trousers and army boots, and he was wearing the mirrored sunglasses, though it was night. Angie was led to a second chair only a few feet away from the commandant; her friends, however, were ignored. King Kosongo was not present, but his wives were crowded into their usual place, standing behind the tree under the watchful eye of the old sadist with the bamboo stick.

The "army" was present: the Leopard brotherhood with their rifles and the Bantu guards armed with machetes, knives, and clubs. The men of the local tribe were very young, and they gave the impression of being as frightened as the rest of the inhabitants of the village. The foreigners soon found out why.

The three musicians in their costume of military jackets *sans* trousers, the ones who had beat sticks the night Kate and her group arrived, now were in charge of the drums. The sound they produced was monotonous, melancholy, and menacing, very different from the Pygmies' music. The *bom-bom-bom* went on a long time, until the moon added its light to that of the torches. In the meanwhile, plastic containers and gourds filled with palm wine were being passed from hand to hand. This time the wine was offered to women, children, and visitors. The commandant was drinking American whisky, undoubtedly obtained from smugglers. He drank a couple of sips and passed the bottle to Angie, who rejected the offer with dignity because she didn't want to establish any basis of familiarity with that man. When he offered her a cigarette, however, she couldn't resist; she hadn't smoked for an eternity.

At a gesture from Mbembelé, the musicians pounded their drums to announce the start of the event. At the far end of the plaza, the two guards were brought in who had been assigned to watch the foreigners' building but had let Nadia and Alexander escape right beneath their noses. They were pushed into the outlined square where they dropped to their knees, trembling, heads hanging. Kate calculated that they were about her grandson's age, maybe seventeen or eighteen. A woman, perhaps one of their mothers, screamed and ran toward the ring but immediately was held back by other women, who put their arms around her and led her away, trying to console her.

Mbembelé rose to his feet and took a pose: legs apart, fists on his hips, jaw protruding, sweat gleaming on his shaved head and naked athletic torso. In that posture and with the dark sunglasses hiding his eyes, he looked exactly like an action film villain. He barked a few phrases in his language, which the visitors did not understand, and immediately threw himself back into his chair. A soldier handed a knife to each of the young men inside the square.

The rules of the game were quickly apparent to Kate and her party. The two guards' sentence was to fight for their lives; their companions, along with their family and friends, were sentenced to witness that inhuman penalty. *Ezenji*, the sacred dance, which the Pygmies had once performed before going out on the hunt to invoke the great spirit of the forest, had degenerated in Ngoubé to become a tourney of death.

· · ·

The contest between the two guards was brief. For a few minutes, they seemed to dance in circles, daggers in hand, watching for a careless move from their opponent that would allow them to strike a blow. While Mbembelé and his soldiers egged them on with yells and whistles, the remaining spectators were ominously silent. The Bantus were terrorized; they realized that any one of them could be the next to be sentenced. The people of Ngoubé, impotent and furious, silently said their good-byes. Only their fear of Mbembelé and intoxication from the palm wine prevented a revolt. Families were united through multiple blood ties; everyone watching the horrible tournament was a relative of the two young men with the daggers.

When at last the combatants attacked, their blades glinted an instant in the light of the torches before flashing downward. Two simultaneous screams rent the night. Both fell; one rolled about on the ground and the other landed on all fours, still clutching his weapon. The moon seemed to stop in the sky as Ngoubé held its breath. Long minutes passed. The youth on the ground shuddered a few times then lay motionless. The other contestant dropped his knife and huddled with his forehead touching the ground and his arms around his head, convulsed with tears.

Mbembelé stood, and with conscious deliberation walked to the ring. With the tip of his boot he turned over the body of the youth on the ground, then unsheathed the pistol he wore at his waist and aimed at the head of the other combatant. In that instant Angie Ninderera threw herself into the center of the plaza and grabbed the commandant so swiftly and so forcefully that she caught him off guard. The bullet buried itself in the ground a few inches from the head of the "victor." An exhalation of horror ran through the crowd: It was absolutely forbidden to touch the commandant. No one, ever, had dared oppose him that way. Mbembelé was so stunned by what Angie had done that it was several seconds before he could recover, which gave her time to position herself in front of the pistol, blocking a second shot.

"Tell King Kosongo that I agree to be his wife, and that I want the lives of these men as a wedding present," she said in a firm voice.

Mbembelé and Angie stared into each other's eyes, taking one another's measure like a pair of boxers before a match. The commandant was half a head taller and much stronger than she. In addition, he had a pistol, but Angie was one of those persons who have indestructible self-confidence. She thought of herself as beautiful, clever, and irresistible; and she had a bold way about her that helped her get anything her heart desired. She placed her hands on the naked chest of the despised commandant—touching him for the second time—and gave him a gentle shove, obliging him to step back. Then she dazzled him with a smile that would undo the most ferocious of men.

"Come on, Commandant. Now I will accept a drink of your whisky," she said cheerfully, as if she had witnessed a circus act and not a duel to the death.

In the meantime, Brother Fernando, followed by Kate and Joel, had gone to the ring and picked up the two young men. One was covered in blood and unsteady on his feet; the other was unconscious. They put both men's arms around their shoulders and literally dragged them to the hut where they were sequestered, while the entire population of Ngoubé, the Bantu guards, and the Brotherhood of the Leopard observed the scene with unparalleled astonishment.

CHAPTER THIRTEEN

David and Goliath

❖

QUEEN NANA-ASANTE ACCOMPANIED NADIA and Alexander along the narrow trail through the jungle that joined the village of the ancestors with the altar where Beyé-Dokou was waiting. The sun wasn't yet up, and the moon had disappeared. It was the blackest hour of the night, but Alexander had his flashlight and Nana-Asante knew the path by heart; she had traveled it many times to pick up the offerings of food left by the Pygmies.

Alexander and Nadia were transformed by their experience in the world of the spirits. For a few hours they had ceased to be individuals and had melded into the absolute of existence. They felt strong, secure, clearheaded: They saw reality from a richer and more luminous perspective. They had left fear behind, including fear of death; now they understood that, happen what may, they would not be swallowed up by darkness. They would never be separated; they were part of a single spirit.

It was difficult for them to imagine that on the metaphysical plane, evil people like Mauro Carías in the Amazon, the Specialist in the Forbidden Kingdom, and Kosongo in Ngoubé had souls identical to theirs. How was it possible that there was no difference between villains and heroes, saints and criminals, between those who do good and those who pass through the world sowing destruction and pain? They didn't know the answer to this mystery, but they conjectured that the experiences of each being contribute to the immense spiritual reserve of the universe. Some do that through the suffering their evil has caused them; others through the light acquired from compassion.

When they returned to the reality of the present, the two young friends thought of the tests that lay ahead. They had one immediate mission to accomplish: to help liberate the slaves and overthrow Kosongo. To do that they had to shatter the indifference of the Bantus; because they hadn't opposed tyranny, they were accomplices to it. There are certain circumstances under which one cannot remain neutral. Alex and Nadia knew, however, that the outcome did not depend on them. The true protagonists and heroes of the story were the Pygmies. That took a tremendous load off their shoulders.

Beyé-Dokou was sleeping and did not hear them arrive. Nadia gently wakened him. When he saw Nana-Asante in the light of the flash, he thought she was a ghost. His eyes bulged and he turned the color of ash, but the queen burst out laughing and rubbed his head to prove that she was as alive as he. Then she told him how all those years she had hidden in the cemetery, not daring to come out because she was afraid of Kosongo. She added that she was tired of waiting for things to change by themselves; the moment had come to go back to Ngoubé, confront the usurper, and free the people from oppression.

"Nadia and I will go ahead to Ngoubé to scout things out," Alexander announced. "We'll arrange to get help. When people know that Nana-Asante is alive, I believe they will find the courage to rebel."

"We hunters come in afternoon," said Beyé-Dokou. "That is hour Kosongo expecting us."

They agreed that Nana-Asante should not come into the village until they were sure that people would back her; otherwise Kosongo would kill her with impunity. She was the one trump card they had to play in this dangerous game; they would leave her for the last. If they could strip Kosongo of his supposedly divine attributes, maybe the Bantus would lose their fear and rise up against him. There were still Mbembelé and his soldiers to contend with, but Alexander and Nadia proposed a plan that was approved by Nana-Asante and Beyé-Dokou. Alexander handed his watch to the queen because the Pygmy didn't know how to use it, and they agreed about the time and the plan of action.

The rest of the hunters joined them. They had spent a good part of the night in ceremonial dancing, asking for help from *Ezenji* and other divinities of the animal and plant worlds. When they saw the queen, their reaction was more extreme than Beyé-Dokou's had been. As one, terrorized, they started running from the "ghost." Beyé-Dokou chased after them, shouting that she was alive, not a wandering soul. Finally, one by one, cautiously, they returned, and dared touch her with the tip of a trembling finger. When they found that she wasn't dead, they welcomed her with respect and hope.

It was Nadia's idea that they should inject King Kosongo with Michael Mushaha's tranquilizer. The day before she had watched one of the hunters drop a monkey using a dart and a blowgun similar to the ones used by the Indians in the Amazon. She didn't see why they couldn't use a dart to deliver the drug. She had no idea what effect it would have on a human. If it could fell a rhinoceros in a few minutes' time, it might kill a human. She assumed, however, that because of Kosongo's enormous size he would survive. His heavy cape would be a problem, however; it acted as almost invincible armor. With the right weapon, one could penetrate the hide of an elephant, but with only a blowgun they would have to hit the target of the king's bare skin.

After Nadia laid out her plan, the Pygmies picked the hunter with the strongest lungs and best aim. The man puffed out his chest and smiled at the distinction they were bestowing on him, but his proud moment did not last long; the rest of the Pygmies burst out laughing and making jokes, the way they always did when someone was prideful. Once the chosen hunter had come back down to earth, they gave him the vial with the tranquilizer. Humbled, he put it in a little pouch at his waist without saying a word.

"The king will sleep like a dead man for several hours. That will give us time to stir the Bantus into action . . . and then we'll produce Queen Nana-Asante," Nadia instructed.

"And what will we do about the commandant and his soldiers?" the hunters asked.

"I will challenge Mbembelé to a contest," said Alexander.

He didn't know why he had said that, or how he would ever carry out such a daring proposition; it was simply the first thing that came to mind, and he blurted it out without thinking. The minute he said it, however, the idea took shape, and he realized that there was no other solution. Just as they had to strip Kosongo of his divinity so people would no longer be afraid of him, so, too, Mbembelé had to be defeated on his own terrain: that of brute force.

"You can't win, Jaguar. You're not like him; you're a peaceful person. Besides, he has firearms, and you've never fired a shot," Nadia argued.

"It won't be a fight with firearms—either hand to hand or with spears."

"You're insane!"

Alexander explained to the hunters that he had a very powerful amulet. He showed them the fossil he wore around his neck and told them that it came from a mythological animal, a dragon that had lived in the high mountains of the Himalayas before human beings walked the earth. That amulet, he said, protected him from cutting objects, and to prove it he told them to stand ten steps from him and attack him with their spears.

The Pygmies put their arms around each other and formed a circle, like a football huddle, chattering like magpies and laughing. From time to time, they sent looks of pity toward the young foreigner who was asking them to do something so crazy. Alexander lost his patience, broke into the middle of the circle, and insisted that they put his claim to the test.

The men took places among the trees, little convinced, and still doubled over with laughter. Alexander measured off ten paces, not a simple task in the middle of so much vegetation, stood in front of them with his hands on his hips, and shouted that he was ready. One by one, the Pygmies threw their spears. Alex did not move a muscle as spearheads whizzed by, hairbreadth from his skin. The hunters, confused, picked up their spears and tried again, this time without laughing and with more concentrated energy, but again they missed their mark.

"Now come after me with machetes," Alexander commanded.

Two of them, the only ones who had machetes, ran toward him shouting at the top of their lungs, but Alex shifted his body only slightly and the blades of the weapons dug into the ground.

"You are a very powerful witch man," they concluded, dumbfounded.

"No, but my amulet is almost as valuable as Ipemba-Afua," Alexander replied.

"You mean that anyone with that amulet can do what you do?" one of the hunters asked.

"Exactly."

Once again the Pygmies formed their circle and whispered excitedly for a long time, until they reached an accord.

"In that case, one of us will fight Mbembelé," they announced.

"Why?" Alexander asked. "I can do it."

"Because you aren't as strong as we are. You are tall, but you don't know how to hunt, and you get tired when you run. Any one of our women is better than you," one of them said.

"Hey! Thanks a lot!"

"It's true." Nadia nodded, hiding a smile.

"The *tuma* will fight Mbembelé," the Pygmies decided.

Everyone was looking at their best hunter, Beyé-Dokou, who meekly refused the honor, as good manners required, although it was easy to see how proud he felt. After he was urged several times to accept, he agreed to hang the dragon amulet around his neck and to stand and face his companion's spears. The earlier scene was repeated, and finally the Pygmies were convinced that the fossil was an impenetrable shield. Alexander visualized the tiny, child-sized Beyé-Dokou facing the imposing Mbembelé.

"Do you know the story of David and Goliath?" he asked.

"No," the Pygmies replied.

"Long, long ago, far away from this forest, two tribes were at war. One of them had a champion called Goliath, who was a giant as tall as a tree and as strong as an elephant. His sword weighed as much as ten machetes. Everyone was terrified of him. David, a boy in the other tribe, was brave enough to challenge him. His weapons were a slingshot and a stone. The two tribes gathered to observe the combat. David shot a stone that stuck Goliath in the middle of his forehead, and he fell to the ground. Then David took his sword away and killed him."

The listeners doubled over laughing. To them the story was incomparably comic, but they didn't see the parallel until Alexander explained that Goliath was Mbembelé and their David was Beyé-Dokou. Too bad they didn't have a sling, the Pygmies said. They had no idea what a sling was, but they imagined it to be a formidable weapon. Finally it was time for the new friends to be on their way toward Ngoubé. They said good-bye, after clapping Alex and Nadia on the arms again and again, and disappeared into the forest.

Alexander and Nadia entered the village just as it was beginning to dawn. Only a few dogs noticed them; the villagers were sleeping and no one was guarding the former mission. They peered into the hut with caution, not wanting to startle their friends, and were greeted by Kate, who had slept very little and very poorly. When she saw her grandson, the writer felt a mixture of profound relief and a desire to give him a sound whipping. All she could do, however, was grab him by the ear and shake him, berating him all the while.

"Where were you two, you devilish brats?" she yelled.

Alexander laughed. "I love you, too, Grandmother," he said, and gave her a big hug.

"I mean it this time, Alexander. I'm never going anywhere with you again! And as for you, missy, you have a lot of explaining to do!" she added, turning to Nadia.

Her grandson interrupted. "This isn't the time to go all mushy, Kate; we have a lot to accomplish."

By then everyone in the hut was awake and standing around Alex and Nadia, besieging them with questions. Kate got tired of mouthing recriminations no one was listening to, so instead she decided to offer the newly arrived youngsters something to eat. She pointed out the mounds of pineapples, mangos, and bananas, vessels filled with chicken fried in palm oil, cassava pudding, and vegetables, all of which had been brought as gifts. Alex and Nadia wolfed them down gratefully; they had eaten very little for the last two days. For dessert, Kate gave them her last can of peaches.

"Didn't I tell you the youngsters would be back? Praise be to God!" Brother Fernando kept repeating.

In one corner of the hut, they had made a place for the guards whose lives Angie had saved. One of them, named Adrien, was dying from the knife in his stomach. The other, called Nzé, was wounded in the chest, but according to the missionary, who had seen many wounds in the war in Rwanda, no vital organ was compromised and he could recover—unless the wound became infected. He had lost a lot of blood, but he was young and strong. Brother Fernando bandaged him up the best he could and was giving him antibiotics from the store Angie carried in her first-aid kit.

"It's good that you kids got back. We have to get out of here before Kosongo claims me as a wife," Angie told Alex and Nadia.

"We will do that with the Pygmies' help, but first we have to help them," Alexander replied. "This afternoon the hunters will come. The plan is to unmask Kosongo and then challenge Mbembelé."

"Sounds like taking candy from a baby," Kate said sarcastically. "But how are you going to do it?"

Alexander and Nadia explained the strategy, which included, among other points, engaging the Bantus, telling them that Queen Nana-Asante was alive, and setting the slave women free so they could fight along with their men.

"Does anyone here know how we can disable the soldiers' rifles?" Alexander asked.

"You have to jam the firing mechanism," Kate said.

It occurred to the writer that they could do that with the resin used to light the torches, a thick, sticky substance kept stored in tin drums in each of the huts. The only persons with free access to the soldiers' barracks were the Pygmy slave women charged with cleaning, carrying water, and preparing food. Nadia offered to direct that operation, since she had already established contact with them when she visited their corral. Kate picked up Angie's rifle to explain where to put the resin.

Brother Fernando told them that Nzé, one of the two wounded Bantus, could also help. His mother, along with Adrien's mother and other family members, had come the night before bringing gifts of fruit, food, palm wine, and even tobacco for Angie. She had become the local heroine for being the only person in their history who had stood up to the commandant. She not only had talked back to him, she had touched him. The villagers didn't know how they could repay her for having saved Adrien and Nzé from certain death at the hands of Mbembelé.

Adrien was expected to die at any moment, but Nzé was lucid, though very weak. The terrible tourney had shaken him from the paralysis of terror he had lived in for years. He felt reborn; fate was offering him a few more days of life as a gift. He had nothing to lose, since he was as good as dead. As soon as the strangers left, Mbembelé would throw him to the crocodiles. By accepting the possibility of imminent death, he gained a courage he had not had before. That bravery was redoubled when he learned that Queen Nana-Asante was going to return to reclaim the throne Kosongo had usurped. He accepted the strangers' plan to incite the Bantus of Ngoubé, but he asked that if the plan did not turn out as expected, they promise to give Adrien and him a merciful death. They did not want to fall into Mbembelé's hands alive.

• • •

Later that morning Kate called on the commandant to inform him that Nadia and Alexander had miraculously escaped death in the forest and were back in the village. That meant that she and the rest of her group would be leaving as soon as the canoes came the next day to pick them up. She added that she was very disappointed that she had not been able to interview His Most Serene Majesty, King Kosongo, for her magazine.

The commandant seemed relieved to learn that the bothersome foreigners would be leaving his territory, and he was willing to help them as long as Angie kept her promise to take her place in King Kosongo's harem. Kate had feared that would happen, and she had a story ready. She asked where the king was. Why hadn't they seen him? Was he ill? She hoped that the sorcerer who meant to marry Angie Ninderera hadn't put a curse on him from across all that distance. Everyone knew that the betrothed or the wife of a witch man is untouchable. And this was a particularly vengeful man, she said. Once before when an important politician had insisted on paying court to Angie, he had lost his position in government, his health, and his fortune. Desperate, he had paid some hirelings to murder the sorcerer, but they hadn't succeeded because their machetes melted like butter in their hands, she added.

Perhaps Mbembelé was impressed with her story, but Kate couldn't tell because she couldn't read his expression behind the mirrored glasses.

"This afternoon His Majesty King Kosongo will preside over a celebration in honor of the woman and the ivory the Pygmies will be bringing," he announced.

"Forgive me, Commandant, but isn't dealing in ivory outlawed?" Kate asked.

"Ivory, and every product here, belongs to the king. Is that understood, old woman?"

"Understood, Commandant."

In the meantime, Nadia, Alexander, and the others in the *International Geographic* group were making their preparations. Angie couldn't help, as she wanted, because four of the king's young wives came to get her and take her to the river, where they kept her company during a long bath overseen by the old man with the bamboo stick. When he raised his arm to administer a few preventative canings to his master's future wife, Angie laid him out flat in the mud with a right to the chin. Then she broke the bamboo over one ample knee and threw the pieces in his face, with the warning that the next time he lifted a hand to her she would dispatch him to the land of his ancestors. The four girls were overcome with such a fit of laughing that they had to sit down; their legs wouldn't hold them. Awed, they felt Angie's muscles and realized that if this husky woman entered the harem their lives might possibly take a turn for the better. Perhaps Kosongo had at last met an opponent who was his equal.

As for Nadia, she was instructing Beyé-Dokou's wife, Jena, how to disable the rifles with the resin. Once Jena understood what was expected of her, she trotted off with her tiny little girl steps toward the soldiers' barracks without further questions or comments. She was so small and insignificant, so quiet and discreet, that no one noticed the fierce gleam of vengeance in her chestnut-colored eyes.

Brother Fernando learned the fate of the missing missionaries through Nzé. Though he had suspected it, the shock of finding his fears confirmed was traumatic. The missionaries had come to Ngoubé for the purpose of spreading their faith, and nothing could dissuade them, not threats, not the hellish climate, not the solitude in which they lived. Kosongo had kept them well isolated, but gradually they had begun to win the confidence of a few villagers, which brought down the

wrath of the king and Mbembelé. When they overtly
began to oppose the abuse suffered by the Bantus and
to intercede for the Pygmy slaves, the commandant put
them and their belongings into a canoe and shipped
them off downriver. A week later, however, the brothers returned, more determined than ever. Within a few
days they disappeared. The official version was that
they had never been in Ngoubé. The soldiers burned
the few things they owned, and it was forbidden to
speak their names. It was no mystery to anyone, however, that the missionaries had been murdered, and that
their bodies had been thrown into the pond of the
crocodiles. No trace of them remained.

"They're martyrs, true saints; they will never be forgotten," Brother Fernando promised, drying the tears
running down his gaunt cheeks.

At about three P.M. Angie returned. She was nearly
unrecognizable. Her hair was combed into a tower of
curls and gold and glass beads that brushed the ceiling.
Her skin was gleaming with oil and she was dressed in
snakeskin sandals and a voluminous tunic of bold
colors. She wore gold bracelets from wrist to elbow.
Her arrival filled the hut.

"She looks like the Statue of Liberty!" Nadia commented, enchanted.

"God almighty, woman! What have they done to

you?" the horrified missionary exclaimed.

"Nothing that can't be undone, Brother," she replied and, jingling her gold bracelets, she added, "With all this I can buy a whole fleet of planes."

"That is, if you escape from Kosongo."

"We're all going to escape, Brother." She smiled, very sure of herself.

"Not all of us. I'm staying to take the place of the brothers who were murdered," the missionary replied.

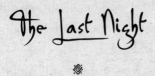

CHAPTER FOURTEEN

The Last Night

THE FESTIVITIES BEGAN ABOUT FIVE in the afternoon, when it was a little less hot. A climate of great tension hovered over Ngoubé. Nzé's mother had spread the word among the Bantus that Nana-Asante, the legitimate queen, greatly mourned by her people, was alive. She added that the foreigners were planning to help the queen recover her throne, and that this would be the last chance they had to free themselves of Kosongo and Mbembelé. How long were they going to put up with his recruiting their sons to turn them into murderers? They were spied on every minute, with no freedom to move about or think, and they were poorer every day. Everything they produced, Kosongo took away. While he was piling up gold, diamonds, and ivory, the people could not get basic medical care. The woman spoke in secret with her daughters, the daughters told their women friends, and in less than an hour most of the adults shared the general restlessness. They didn't dare enlist the guards, even though they were members of their own families; they didn't know how they would react. Mbembelé had brainwashed them; he held them in his fist.

The anxiety was greater still among the Pygmy women because that afternoon the allotted time would run out for saving their children. Their husbands had always managed to come up with the elephant tusks in time, but now something was different. Nadia had given Jena the fabulous news that their magic amulet, Ipemba-Afua, had been recovered, and that the men were coming not with ivory but with a determination to confront Kosongo. The women would have to fight with the men. They had borne their slavery for years, believing that their families would survive if they obeyed. Their submission had yielded little fruit, however; their living conditions grew steadily worse. The more they put up with, the worse the abuse they suffered. As Jena explained to the other women, when there were no more elephants in the forest, Mbembelé and Kosongo would sell their children anyway. Better to die rebelling than live in slavery.

Kosongo's harem was also in an uproar because they had found out that the king's future wife was not afraid of anything and was almost as strong as Mbembelé; she had mocked the king and had knocked the old man down with one punch. The women who hadn't been lucky enough to witness that scene couldn't believe it. They were afraid of Kosongo, who had forced them to marry him, and they had a healthy respect for the crotchety old man who had the task of guarding them. Some believed that the arrogant Angie Ninderera would be tamed in less than three days and would become one of the most submissive of the king's wives—that's what had happened to them—but the four young women who had gone with her to the river, and who had seen her muscles and her attitude, were convinced that wouldn't happen.

The only ones unaware that something was brewing were precisely those who should have been best informed: Mbembelé and his "army." Authority had gone to their heads; they felt invincible. They had created their own reality, in which they felt comfortable, and since no one had ever defied them, they had grown careless.

By Mbembelé's orders, the women of the village were put in charge of preparations for the king's wedding. They decorated the square with a hundred torches and arches fashioned from palm branches. They piled up pyramids of fruit and assembled a banquet with what they had at hand: hens, rats, lizards, antelope, cassava, and corn. Containers of palm wine began to circulate among the guards early on, but the civilian population abstained, just as Nzé's mother had instructed them.

Everything was ready for the dual ceremony of the royal wedding and the delivery of the ivory. It was still twilight, but the torches were already lit and the odor of roast meat was heavy on the air. Mbembelé's soldiers and his pathetic court were lined up beneath the Tree of Words. All of Ngoubé was crowded along both sides of the square, and the Bantu guards were standing at their posts, armed with machetes and clubs. Wood stools had been provided for the foreign visitors. Joel had his cameras loaded, and the rest of the *International Geographic* group was on the alert, ready to act when the moment came. Nadia was the only one of the group missing.

Angie Ninderera was waiting in a place of honor beneath the tree, looking impressive in her new tunic and gold ornaments. She did not seem in the least worried, despite the many things that could go wrong that evening. When Kate had outlined her fears earlier that morning, Angie had replied that the man who could frighten her had yet to be born, and she added that Kosongo would soon see who she was.

"It won't be long until the king offers me all his gold just to get me out of here." She laughed.

"Unless he throws you into the pond with the crocodiles," muttered Kate, who was highly nervous.

When the hunters arrived in the village carrying their nets and spears, but without elephant tusks, the inhabitants realized that the tragedy had been set in motion and nothing could stop it. A long, collective sigh traveled around the square. In a way people felt relieved; anything was better than suffering the horrible tension of that day any longer. The Bantu guards, confused, surrounded the Pygmies, awaiting instructions from their chief, but the commandant was nowhere to be found.

A half hour dragged by, during which anxiety increased to an unbearable level. The containers of liquor circulated among the young guards, whose eyes by now were bloodshot, and who had become talkative and disorderly. One of the Leopard Brotherhood barked a command at them, and they immediately put down the palm wine and stood at attention, but that did not last long.

A martial drum roll finally announced the arrival of the king. The march was led by The Royal Mouth, accompanied by a guard carrying a basket of heavy gold jewelry as a gift for the bride. Kosongo could afford to appear generous in public because as soon as Angie became part of his harem, the so-called gifts would be returned to him. Next came the wives; they, too, covered in gold. The old man who supervised them trailed along behind, face swollen and with only four loose teeth in his head. A notable change was evident in the attitude of the women, who were acting more like a herd of frisky zebras than sheep. Angie waved, and they answered with broad smiles of complicity.

Behind the harem came the throne-bearers carrying the platform on which Kosongo was seated in his French armchair throne. He was wearing the same garb they had seen before, including the impressive hat with the beaded curtain that covered his face. His mantle appeared to be scorched in several places, but wearable. The Pygmies' amulet was missing from Kosongo's staff, and in its place was a similar bone that from a distance could pass as Ipemba-Afua. It did not befit a king to admit that a sacred object had been stolen from him. Beyond that, he was confident that he didn't need the amulet to control the Pygmies, whom he considered to be as low as the beasts of the jungle.

The royal procession came to a halt in the middle of the square, so everyone would have a chance to admire the sovereign. Before the porters carried the platform to its place beneath the Tree of Words, The Royal Mouth asked the Pygmies to present the ivory. The hunters stepped forward, and the entire village could see that one of them was carrying the sacred amulet, Ipemba-Afua.

Beyé-Dokou made his announcement in a steady voice: "The elephants are gone. We cannot bring more tusks. Now we want our women and our children. We are going back to the forest."

That brief speech was met with sepulchral silence. The possibility that the slaves might rebel had never occurred to anyone. The first instinct of the soldiers of the Leopard Brotherhood was to shoot the entire crew of hunters, but Mbembelé wasn't there to give the order, and the king still had not reacted. The population was caught off guard because Nzé's mother hadn't told them anything about the Pygmies. For years the Bantus had benefited from the slaves' labors and it was definitely not to their advantage to lose them, but they understood that the equilibrium of the past had been broken. For the first time, they felt respect for these little people—the poorest, most defenseless, and vulnerable in the forest—for showing unbelievable courage.

Kosongo waved over his spokesman and whispered

something into his ear. The Royal Mouth passed on the order to bring in the children. Six guards went to one of the corrals and shortly afterward reappeared leading a wretched little group: two elderly women dressed in raffia skirts, each with babies in her arms, surrounded by children of various ages, tiny and terrorized. When they saw their parents, some gave an indication of running to them, but they were stopped by the guards.

"The king must do business; it is his duty," announced The Royal Mouth. "You know what happens if you do not bring ivory."

Kate Cold could not bear the anguish any longer, and although she had promised Alexander that she wouldn't intervene, she ran to the middle of the square and stopped right in front of the royal platform, which was still on the shoulders of the bearers. Forgetting everything about protocol, which demanded that she prostrate herself, she started yelling insults at Kosongo, reminding him that they were international journalists and that they would tell the world about the crimes against humanity that were taking place in this village. She wasn't allowed to finish as two soldiers armed with rifles lifted her off her feet. She kept shouting, feet kicking in the air, as they carried her off toward the site of the crocodiles.

• • •

The plan that Nadia and Alexander had sketched out with such care collapsed in a matter of minutes. They had assigned a responsibility to each member of the group, but Kate's untimely intervention sowed chaos among the friends. Fortunately the guards, indeed all those present, were confused.

The Pygmy designated to shoot the king with the ampoule of tranquilizer had hidden among the huts, but now he couldn't wait for his best shot. Hurried by circumstances, he put the blowgun to his mouth and blew, but the dart intended for Kosongo hit the chest of one of the bearers carrying the platform. The man felt something like a bee sting but he didn't have a free hand to brush away what he thought was an insect. For a few instants, nothing happened, then suddenly his knees buckled and he fell to the ground unconscious. The other bearers were not prepared, and the weight of the platform was too great for them to hold; it tilted and the French armchair slid toward the ground. Kosongo gave a yell, trying to keep his balance, and for a fraction of a second he was suspended in air. Then he crashed, tangled in his mantle, hat askew and bawling with rage.

Angie Ninderera decided that the time had come to

improvise, since the original plan had gone awry. With four long strides she reached the fallen king; she swept aside the guards trying to hold her back and, voicing one of her loud Comanche yells, she grabbed the king's hat and jerked it off the royal head.

Angie's action was so unexpected, and so daring, that everyone was stopped in place, as if posed for a photograph. The ground didn't tremble when the king's feet touched it. His cries of rage had not left anyone deaf; birds hadn't dropped from the skies, nor had the jungle convulsed in its final death rattles. Looking upon Kosongo's face for the first time, no one was blinded . . . only dumbfounded. When the hat and the curtain fell aside, what everyone could see was the unmistakable head of Commandant Maurice Mbembelé.

"Kate said that you two looked too much alike!" Angie exclaimed.

By then the soldiers had reacted and rushed to surround the commandant, but no one dared touch him. Even the men who were dragging Kate to her death released the writer and ran to their chief, but they, too, were afraid to help him. Finally Mbembelé succeeded in untangling himself from his mantle and with one motion leaped to his feet. He was the image of fury: streaming sweat, eyes bulging out of his head, foaming at the mouth, roaring like an enraged beast. He lifted one gigantic fist with the intention of pounding Angie into the ground, but she was already out of reach.

Beyé-Dokou chose that moment to step forward. It took enormous bravery to defy the commandant in normal times. To do so now when he was so indignant was suicidal. The tiny hunter looked insignificant facing the enormous Mbembelé, who rose like a tower before him. Looking up, way up, the Pygmy challenged the giant to compete in one-on-one combat.

A hum of amazement ran through the crowd. No one could believe what they were seeing. People crowded closer, pressing behind the Pygmies, and the guards, as surprised as the rest of the population, could not hold them back.

Mbembelé hesitated, caught off guard, as the slave's words penetrated his brain. When finally he comprehended the outlandish daring that such a challenge implied, he erupted in thunderous laughter that spread out like waves for several minutes. The soldiers of the Brotherhood imitated him; they felt it was expected of them, but their laughter was forced. Events had become too grotesque, and they didn't know what to do. The hostility of the villagers was tangible, and they could sense that the Bantu guards were confused and near rebellion.

"Clear the square!" ordered Mbembelé.

The concept of *Ezenji*, or a hand-to-hand duel, was not new to anyone in Ngoubé; that was how prisoners were punished and, in the process, a diversion was created that the commandant found entertaining. The only difference in this case was that Mbembelé would not be judge and spectator; he would himself be a participant. Obviously fighting a Pygmy did not give him a moment's worry; he would crush him like a worm, but first he would make him suffer.

Brother Fernando, who had kept a certain distance all this time, now came to the front, cloaked in a new authority. The news of his companions' deaths had reinforced his faith and his courage. He didn't fear Mbembelé, because he harbored the conviction that sooner or later evil beings pay for their sins, and the commandant had amply filled his quota of crimes. The time had come to render accounts.

"I will act as referee. You may not use firearms. What weapons do you choose, spear, knife, or machete?" he asked.

"None of them. We will fight without weapons, hand to hand," the commandant replied. His expression was truly ferocious.

Beyé-Dokou did not hesitate. "Fine," he said.

Alexander knew that his friend believed he was protected by the fossil. He didn't know that it would serve only against cutting weapons and would not shield him from the commandant's superhuman strength. He would tear him apart with his bare hands. Alex led Brother Fernando aside to plead with him not to accept those conditions, but the missionary replied that God watched over the cause of the just.

"Beyé-Dokou won't have a chance! The commandant is much, much stronger!" Alexander exclaimed.

"As the bull is much stronger than the torero. The trick is to wear the beast down," the missionary indicated.

Alexander opened his mouth to reply but instantly understood what Brother Fernando was trying to tell him. He shot off to prepare his friend for the tremendous test before him.

At the other end of the village, Nadia had pulled back the bolt and opened the large door to the pen where the Pygmy women were kept. A couple of the hunters who had not gone to the square with the others ran up, bringing spears they distributed among the women, who slipped like ghosts between the huts and took places around the square, hidden by the night shadows, ready to perform their part when called on.

Nadia joined Alexander, who was instructing Beyé-Dokou while the soldiers laid out the ring in the usual place.

"You don't need to worry about the guns, Jaguar, just the pistol Mbembelé wears at his waist. That's the only one we couldn't get to," said Nadia.

"What about the Bantu guards?"

"We don't know how they're going to react, but Kate had an idea," she replied.

"Do you think I should tell Beyé-Dokou that the amulet won't protect him against Mbembelé?" he asked.

"Why?" she replied. "It will just rob him of his confidence."

Alexander noticed that Nadia's voice sounded hoarse, not entirely human; it was almost like a caw. Her eyes were glassy, and she was very pale and breathing hard.

"What's the matter with you, Eagle?" he asked.

"Nothing. Be very careful, Jaguar. I have to go."

"Where?"

"I'm going to look for help against the three-headed monster, Jaguar."

"Remember Má-Bangesé's prophecy! We're supposed to stay together."

Nadia gave him a quick kiss on the forehead and hurried off. In all the excitement going on in the village, no one except Alexander saw the white eagle that rose above the huts and flew out of sight in the direction of the forest.

At one corner of the square stood Commandant Mbembelé. He was barefoot and naked except for the broad leather belt that held his pistol and the shorts he wore beneath the royal mantle. He had rubbed his body with palm oil; his massive muscles looked as if they were sculpted from stone, and his skin gleamed like obsidian in the flickering light of the hundred torches. The ritual scars on his arms and cheeks accentuated his extraordinary appearance. His shaved head looked very small atop his bull neck. The classic features of his face would have been handsome had they not been disfigured by a bestial expression. Despite the loathing the man evoked, no one could help but admire his stupendous physique.

By contrast, the tiny man in the opposite corner was a dwarf; he barely came to the gigantic Mbembelé's waist. There was nothing beautiful about his out-of-proportion limbs and torso, or his flat-nosed face and shortened forehead . . . only the courage and intelligence gleaming in his eyes. He had removed his filthy yellow T-shirt, and he, too, was practically naked and slathered with oil. Around his neck hung a piece of rock on a cord: Alexander's magic dragon dropping.

"A friend of mine named Tensing, who knows more about the art of wrestling than anyone I know, told me that the enemy's strength is also his weakness," Alexander explained to Beyé-Dokou.

"What does that mean?" the Pygmy asked.

"Mbembelé's strength is in his size and his weight. He's like a buffalo, nothing but muscle. Since he weighs so much, he's clumsy and he tires quickly. Besides that, he's arrogant; he isn't accustomed to being challenged. It's been many years since he had to hunt or fight. You are at your best form."

"And I have this," Beyé-Dokou added, stroking the amulet.

"More important that that, my friend," Alexander replied, "is that you are fighting for your life and for the lives of your family. Mbembelé is fighting for pleasure. He's a killer, and like all killers, he's a coward."

Jena, Beyé-Dokou's wife, went to her husband, gave him a brief hug, and said a few words into his ear. At that instant the drums announced the beginning of the fight.

• • •

Around the square lit by torches and moonlight stood the soldiers of the Brotherhood of the Leopard, holding their rifles. Bantu guards made up the second file, and pushing against them were the villagers of Ngoubé, all in a dangerous state of agitation. On orders from Kate, who was not going to lose an opportunity to write a fabulous article for *International Geographic*, Joel was preparing to photograph the event.

Brother Fernando cleaned off his glasses and took off his shirt. His slim, wiry, ascetic's body was a sickly white. Wearing only pants and boots, he was ready to referee, even though he had little hope that he could enforce basic rules of any sort. He realized that he was dealing with a fight to the death, and his deepest desire was to prevent that from happening. He kissed the scapulary around his neck and put his faith in God.

A roar issued from Mbembelé's gut as he lunged forward, making the ground tremble with his footsteps. Beyé-Dokou waited for him, motionless, silent, in exactly his attitude during the hunt: alert, but calm. One of the giant's fists flashed like a cannonball toward the face of the Pygmy, who avoided it by a fraction of an inch. The commandant stumbled past him but immediately recovered his balance. He swung a second time. Again his opponent was not where he had expected, but behind him. These evasions made him furious; he attacked like a crazed beast, but none of his blows touched Beyé-Dokou, who was dancing around the edges of the ring. Every time the giant swung, the Pygmy dodged.

To reach his opponent's squat figure, Mbembelé had to lean down in an uncomfortable stance that drained strength from his arms. If he had landed a single one of his punches, he would have split Beyé-Dokou's head wipe open. He never touched his target, however, because the Pygmy was quick as a gazelle and slippery as a fish. Soon the commandant was panting and blinded by the sweat dripping into his eyes. He concluded that he was going to have to pace himself; he wasn't going to defeat the little man in a single round, as he had thought. Brother Fernando called for a pause, and the husky Mbembelé immediately obeyed, retiring to his corner, where a bucket of water was waiting for him to quench his thirst and wash off the sweat.

Alexander was acting as second for Beyé-Dokou, who danced over to his corner with a wide smile, as if this were a festival. That maddened the commandant, who was watching from across the ring, struggling to get his breath. Beyé-Dokou didn't appear to be thirsty, but he allowed Alex to pour water over his head.

"Your amulet really is magic, the greatest magic there is after Ipemba-Afua," he said with great satisfaction.

"Mbembelé is built like the trunk of a tree; it's difficult for him to bend from the waist, and that's why he doesn't swing downward very well," Alexander explained. "You're doing great, Beyé-Dokou, but you have to tire him even more."

"I know that. He is like the elephant. How can you hunt the elephant if you do not first tire him?"

Alexander felt that the time-out was too short, but Beyé-Dokou was jumping with impatience, and as soon as Brother Fernando gave the signal he bounced to the center of the ring, hopping around like a child. That was a provocation Mbembelé could not let pass. He forgot his resolution to pace himself and roared forward like a truck in high gear. Of course the Pygmy evaded him, and his momentum drove him outside the ring.

Brother Fernando waved his arms vigorously, signaling that he should get back inside the boundaries marked with lime. Mbembelé turned on him, ready to make this insect pay for the impertinence of ordering him around, but a loud protest from all the villagers stopped him. He couldn't believe what he was hearing!

Never, not in his worst nightmares, had the thought passed through his mind that someone would dare contradict him. He couldn't, however, give himself the pleasure of thinking of ways to punish such insolence, for Beyé-Dokou was urging him back into the ring by kicking one of his legs from behind. It was the first contact between them. That little monkey had touched him! *Him!* Commandant Maurice Mbembelé! He swore he would rip him to bits and eat the pieces. That would teach those ridiculous Pygmies a lesson.

Any pretense of following the rules of a clean game disappeared in that instant, and Mbembelé lost control completely. He shoved Brother Fernando out of the way and rushed toward Beyé-Dokou, who suddenly dropped to the ground. Pulling himself into a nearly fetal position, supporting his body on his buttocks, the Pygmy began kicking, landing blow after blow on the giant's legs. For his part, the commandant tried to hit down at him, but Beyé-Dokou was whirling like a top, rolling nimbly to the sides of the ring, making it impossible to catch him. He watched for Mbembelé to pull one foot back to boot him out of the ring, and with all his strength kicked the leg supporting the giant. The enormous human tower of the commandant fell backward. He lay on his back like a cockroach, unable to get up.

By then Brother Fernando had recovered from being shoved aside, had wiped clean his thick eyeglasses, and was again right on top of the battlers. His voice rose above the uproarious shouting of the spectators to proclaim the victor. Alexander jumped into the ring and raised Beyé-Dokou's arm high, shouting with jubilation and echoed by the onlookers—except for the soldiers of the Brotherhood of the Leopard, who had not recovered from their shock.

The village of Ngoubé had never witnessed such a fantastic spectacle. Frankly, by now very few could remember the reason for the contest; they were too excited about the unimaginable fact that the Pygmy had vanquished the giant. That story was instantly part of the legend of the forest; they would tell it for generations to come. Whenever a tree falls, everyone is instantly ready to make firewood. This was the case with Mbembelé, who minutes before was thought to be a demigod. It was an occasion for celebration. The drums began to sound with wild enthusiasm, and the Bantus sang and danced, unconcerned that in those few minutes they had lost their slaves, and that the future was unclear.

The Pygmies slipped between the legs of the guards

and the soldiers, swarmed into the ring, and lifted Beyé-Dokou upon their shoulders. During this out-burst of collective euphoria, Commandant Mbembelé had succeeded in getting to his feet. He grabbed a machete from one of the guards and rushed toward the group triumphantly parading Beyé-Dokou who, now atop the shoulders of his companions, was as tall as the commandant.

No one could ever describe what happened next. Some said that the machete slipped from the comman-dant's oiled and sweaty fingers. Others swore that the blade stopped magically in the air an inch from Beyé-Dokou's neck and then flew through the air as if whirled away by a hurricane. Whatever the cause, the fact is that the crowd was immobilized, and Mbembelé, seized by superstitious terror, whipped a knife from another guard and hurled it at his opponent. His aim was off, however, because Joel had run up to shoot a photograph and blinded him with the flash.

At that point Commandant Mbembelé ordered his soldiers to fire upon the Pygmies. Everyone scattered, screaming. Women pulled their children away, old people tripped in their haste, dogs fled, hens flapped in circles, and finally no one was left but the Pygmies, the soldiers, and the guards, who couldn't decide whose side to take. Kate and Angie ran to protect the screaming Pygmy children, who were huddled around the two grandmothers' feet like pups. Joel dove beneath the table that held the feast for the nuptial banquet and blindly shot photographs in every direction. Brother Fernando and Alexander placed themselves with outspread arms in front of the Pygmies, protecting them with their bodies.

Perhaps some of the soldiers tried to shoot and found that their weapons were disabled. Maybe others, disgusted at the cowardice of the chief they had until then respected, refused to obey. In either case, not a single bullet was fired. One instant later, each of the ten soldiers of the Brotherhood of the Leopard felt the tip of a spear against his throat: The quiet Pygmy women had swung into action.

Mbembelé, blind with rage, saw nothing of this. All that registered was that his orders had been ignored. He drew his pistol from his waist, aimed at Beyé-Dokou, and fired. He didn't know that the bullet missed the target, deflected by the magical power of the amulet, because before he could get off a second shot an animal he had never seen, an enormous black cat, leaped upon him; it had the speed and fierceness of a leopard and the yellow eyes of a panther.

CHAPTER FIFTEEN

The Three-Headed Monster

❖

EVERYONE WHO WATCHED THE YOUNG foreigner's transformation into a black feline realized that this was the most amazing night of their lives. Their language lacked words to recount such marvels; they did not even have a name for that unfamiliar animal, a great black cat that roared as it charged the commandant. The beast's hot breath struck Mbembelé in the face, and its claws dug into his shoulders. He could have killed the feline with one shot, but he was paralyzed with terror; he realized he had encountered a supernatural beast, a wondrous feat of witchcraft. He escaped the jaguar's lethal embrace by pummeling it with both fists and ran desperately toward the forest, followed by the beast. Both disappeared into the darkness, leaving witnesses stunned by what they had seen.

All the Bantus of Ngoubé, along with the Pygmies, lived a magical reality, surrounded with spirits, always fearful of violating a taboo or committing an offense that might unleash hidden forces. They believed that illnesses were caused by sorcery and could, therefore, be cured in the same way, that they should never hunt or travel without first performing a ceremony to placate the gods, that the night is peopled with demons and the day with ghosts, and that the dead turn into flesh eaters. To them the physical world was very mysterious, and life itself a kind of spell. They had seen—or they believed they had seen—many examples of witchcraft, and therefore did not think it impossible that a person could turn into a beast. There were two explanations: Alexander was a very powerful sorcerer, or else he was the spirit of an animal that had temporarily taken the form of a human.

The transformation was quite a different matter for Brother Fernando, who was standing close to Alexander when he metamorphosed into his totemic animal. The missionary, who prided himself on being a rational European, a person of education and culture, saw what happened, but his mind couldn't accept it. He removed his eyeglasses and wiped them against his trousers. "I definitely have to change these lenses," he muttered, rubbing his eyes. There were explanations for Alexander's having disappeared at the same instant the enormous cat appeared out of nowhere: It was night, there was tremendous confusion in the square, the light of the torches was untrustworthy, and he himself was in a very emotional state. He didn't have time to waste in futile conjectures; he decided. There was too much to do. The Pygmies—men and women—had the soldiers at the tips of their spears or immobilized in their nets; the Bantu guards were vacillating between throwing down their weapons and going to the aid of their chiefs; the people of Ngoubé were near rebelling; and there was a climate of hysteria that could degenerate into a massacre if the guards decided to help Mbembelé's soldiers.

Alexander returned a few minutes later. Only the strange expression on his face, the incandescent eyes and menacing teeth, indicated his recent pursuits. An excited Kate ran to meet him

"Alex! Alex! You'll never believe what happened! A black panther attacked Mbembelé. I hope he gobbled him up; it's the least he deserves."

"It wasn't a panther, Kate. It was a jaguar. It didn't eat him, but it gave him a good scare."

"How do you know that?"

"How many times do I have to tell you that my totemic animal is the jaguar, Kate?'

"Still harping on that same old obsession, Alexander! You are going to have to see a psychiatrist when we get back to civilization. Where's Nadia?"

"She'll be back soon."

During the next half hour the delicate balance of forces in the village was on the way to being defined, thanks in large part to Brother Fernando, Kate, and Angie. The missionary was able to convince the soldiers of the Brotherhood of the Leopard that they should surrender if they wanted to get out of Ngoubé alive. Their weapons wouldn't fire, they had lost their commandant, and they were surrounded by a hostile population.

In the meanwhile, Kate and Angie had gone to the hut to look for Nzé and, with the help of the wounded man's family, had brought him there on an improvised stretcher. The former guard was burning with fever, but after his mother explained what had taken place that evening, he wanted to help. They set him down in a visible spot, where in a weak but clear voice he spoke to his companions, urging them to rebel. There was nothing to fear; Mbembelé was out of the picture. The guards wanted to go back to a normal life with their families, but they felt a deep-seated fear of the commandant, and were programmed to obey his authority. Where was he? Had the ghost of the large cat devoured him? But if they listened to Nzé and then their leader returned, they would end up in the pond of the crocodiles. They didn't believe that Queen Nana-Asante was alive, and even if she was, her power could not compare to that of Mbembelé.

Once they were reunited with their families, the Pygmies were ready to head back to the forest, which they never meant to leave again. Beyé-Dokou donned his yellow T-shirt, picked up his spear, and went over to Alexander to return the fossil he believed had saved him from being ground to mush by Mbembelé. The other hunters also said their emotional good-byes, knowing they would not see this wonderful friend with the spirit of a great cat again. Alexander stopped them. They couldn't go quite yet, he told them. He explained that they wouldn't be safe, even in the deepest heart of the jungle where no other human could survive. Running wasn't the solution, since sooner or later the world would catch up with them or they would need that contact. They had to deliver the last blow to slavery and to reestablish the friendly relations they once had with the people of Ngoubé, which meant they had to rob Mbembelé of his power and chase him and his soldiers from the region forever.

As for Kosongo's wives, who had been kept prisoner

in his harem from the age of fourteen or fifteen, they had mutinied, and for the first time were enjoying being young. Oblivious to much more serious matters worrying the rest of the population, they had organized their own carnival: They were playing the drums, singing and dancing. They tore the gold ornaments from their arms, throats, and ears and tossed them into the air, wild with their new freedom.

That was the state of events in the village—everyone still in the square but each group absorbed in its own concerns—when Sombe made his spectacular appearance, summoned by occult forces to impose order, punishment, and terror.

A rain of sparks like fireworks announced the arrival of the formidable sorcerer. The dreaded entrance was welcomed with a single outcry. Sombe had not materialized in many months, and some had harbored the hope that he had gone to the world of the demons for all time. But there he was, the messenger from all that is evil, more impressive and filled with fury than ever. People backed away, horrified, as he took the center of the square.

Sombe's fame had spread beyond the region, and village by village it had traveled across much of Africa.

It was said that he could kill with his thoughts, cure with a breath, divine the future, manipulate nature, alter dreams, sink mortals into a sleep of no return, and communicate with the gods. It was also told that he was invincible and immortal, that he could turn himself into any creature of sea, sky, or earth, and that he entered the bodies of his enemies and devoured them from within. He drank their blood, turned their bones to powder, and left nothing but skin, which he then filled with ashes. That was how he created zombies, the living dead whose horrendous fate was to serve him as slaves.

The sorcerer was gigantic, and his incredible attire seemed to double his stature. His face was covered with a leopard mask and, in place of a hat, he wore a large-horned buffalo skull crowned in turn with a leafy branch, as if a tree were sprouting from his head. His arms and legs were adorned with the teeth and claws of wild beasts, and he had a necklace of human fingers. Around his waist a string of fetishes and gourds held magic potions. Various animal hides stiff with dried blood cloaked his body.

Sombe arrived with the attitude of a vengeful devil who had determined to impose his personal form of injustice. The Bantu population, the Pygmies, even

Mbembelé's soldiers, submitted without a trace of resistance. They shrank back, trying to disappear, resigned to doing Sombe's will. The foreigners, stunned with surprise, witnessed how his presence destroyed the fragile harmony they had begun to achieve in Ngoubé.

The sorcerer, crouching like a gorilla, roaring, and supporting himself on his hands, began to whirl, faster and faster. Suddenly he would stop and point a finger, and the person he singled out would fall to the ground in a deep trance, shaking with seizures. Some lay rigid, like marble statues, and others began to bleed through the nose, mouth, and ears. Sombe would again spin like a top, stop, and annihilate someone with the power of a gesture. Within a brief time, a dozen men and women were flailing about on the ground, while the rest of the villagers were on their knees, shrieking, eating dirt, begging forgiveness, and swearing obedience.

About them an unexplainable wind blew through the village like a typhoon and, with one blast, lifted the straw from the huts, the food from the banquet table, the drums, the palm arches, and half the hens. The night was bright with a lightning storm, and from the forest came a horrible chorus of moans. Hundreds of rats scurried through the square like a plague and immediately disappeared, leaving a lethal stench in their wake.

Suddenly Sombe leaped into one of the bonfires where meat had been roasting for the feast and began to dance on the burning coals, picking them up with his bare hands to throw into the frightened crowd. From the flames and smoke surged hundreds of demonic figures, legions of evil that accompanied the witch man in his sinister dance. From the buffalo-horned leopard's head thundered a cavernous voice shouting the names of the deposed king and vanquished commandant. The people, hysterical, hypnotized, chorused in return: *Kosongo, Mbembelé, Kosongo, Mbembelé, Kosongo, Mbembelé* . . .

Then, just when the sorcerer had the entire village in the palm of his hand and was triumphantly emerging from the bonfire where flames had been licking his legs—miraculously without burning him—a large white bird appeared in the south and circled the square several times. Alexander shouted with relief as he recognized Nadia.

The eagle had convoked forces that streamed into Ngoubé from the four cardinal points. The gorillas of the jungle led the parade, black and magnificent, great bulls in the lead, followed by the females with their young. Then came Queen Nana-Asante, glorious in the rags barely covering her nakedness, her white hair standing up like a halo of silver. She was riding an enormous elephant as ancient as she, its ribs striped with spear scars. Tensing was there, the lama from the Himalayas who had answered Nadia's call in his astral body, along with his band of fearsome Yetis in war attire. Walimai and the delicate spirit of his wife had brought thirteen fabled mythological beasts with them from the Amazon. Walimai had reverted to his youth, and was once again an impressive warrior arrayed in war paint and feather ornaments. And finally into the village trooped the vast shining throng of the jungle: the ancestors, and spirits of animals and plants, thousands and thousands of souls that lit up the village with the sun of midday and cooled the air with a clean, fresh breeze.

That fantastic light obliterated the evil legions of demons and the sorcerer was reduced to his true size. His bloody hides, his necklaces of human fingers, his fetishes, his claws and teeth, no longer seemed chilling, only a ridiculous disguise. The great elephant Queen Nana-Asante was riding swung its trunk at Sombe's head, sending the buffalo-horned leopard mask flying:

The sorcerer was revealed. Everyone recognized that face! Kosongo, Mbembelé, and Sombe were the same man: the three heads of the same ogre.

The reaction was as unexpected as everything else that happened that strange night. A long, hoarse roar resounded through the tightly packed crowd. Those who had been convulsing, those who had been turned to statues, those who were bleeding, emerged from their trances, and those who lay prostrate got up from the ground, and they all moved as one, with terrifying determination, upon the man who had tyrannized them. Kosongo-Mbembelé-Sombe retreated, but in less than a minute he was surrounded. A hundred hands grasped him, raised him high, and bore him off toward the well of the executions. A bone-tingling howl shook the jungle as the heavy body of the three-headed monster fell into the jaws of the crocodiles.

For Alexander it would be very difficult to remember the details of that night; he couldn't write about them as easily as he had his earlier adventures. Did he dream everything? Was he caught up in the same hysteria that had entrapped all the villagers? Or had he seen with his own eyes the beings Nadia had assembled? He didn't have an answer for those questions.

Later, when he compared his version of events with Nadia's, she listened quietly, then gave him a light kiss on the cheek and told him that each person has his own truth, and that all are valid.

Nadia's words were prophetic, because when he tried to get the true story from other members of the group, each one told him something different. For example, Brother Fernando remembered nothing but the gorillas and an elephant ridden by an ancient woman. Kate seemed to have perceived the glowing bodies in the air, among which she recognized the lama Tensing, although, she said, that was impossible. Joel said he would wait until he could develop his rolls of film before giving an opinion; if it didn't show up in the photographs, it didn't happen. The Pygmies and the Bantus described more or less what he had seen, from the witch man dancing amid the flames to the ancestors flying around Nana-Asante.

Angie captured much more than Alexander had: She saw angels with translucent wings and flocks of bright birds; she heard the music of drums; smelled the perfume of a rain of flowers; and witnessed a number of other miracles. And that was what she told Michael Mushaha when he arrived the next day in a motor launch, looking for them.

One of Angie's radio transmissions had been picked up in his camp, and Michael had immediately set wheels in motion to come after them. He couldn't find a pilot brave enough to fly into the swampy forest in which his friends had been lost; he'd had to take a commercial flight to the capital, rent a launch, and come upriver looking for them with nothing but instinct as a guide. He was accompanied by an official of the national government and four police officers who had been charged with investigating the illegal trade in ivory, diamonds, and slaves.

No one had questioned Nana-Asante's authority, and within a few hours she had restored order to the village. She began by effecting reconciliation between the Bantu population and the Pygmies and reminding them of the importance of cooperation. The Bantus needed the meat the hunters provided, and the little people couldn't live without the products they obtained in Ngoubé. That would force the Bantus to respect their former slaves and be reason for the Pygmies to forgive the mistreatment they had suffered.

"How will you teach them to live in peace?" Kate asked Nana-Asante.

"I will begin with the women," the queen replied. "They have more goodness within them."

• • •

Inevitably, the moment had come for them to leave. The friends were exhausted; they had slept very little, and all of them except Nadia and Borobá were sick to their stomachs. Joel, in addition, had been bitten by mosquitoes from head to foot; the bites had swelled, he had a fever, and he was raw from scratching. Discreetly, avoiding any show of pride or boasting, Beyé-Dokou offered him some of the powder from the sacred amulet. In only a couple of hours, the photographer was back to normal. He was very impressed, and asked for a pinch to cure his friend Timothy Bruce's mandrill bite, but Mushaha informed him that Bruce was totally recovered and waiting for the rest of the team in Nairobi. The Pygmies then applied the same treatment to Adrien and Nzé, who improved right before their eyes. When he witnessed the powers of that mysterious product, Alexander worked up the nerve to ask for a little to take to his mother. According to her physicians, Lisa Cold had conquered her cancer, but her son felt that a few grams of the miraculous green powder from Ipemba-Afua would guarantee her a long life.

Angie Ninderera decided to try to rid herself of her fear of crocodiles by negotiating. She and Nadia peered over the wood-and-vine fence around the well and offered a deal to the monstrous reptiles. Nadia translated to the best of her ability, though her familiarity with saurian tongues was minimal. Angie explained to them that she could shoot and kill them if she wished. Instead, she would lead them to the river where they would be set free. In exchange, she demanded respect for her life. Nadia wasn't sure the creatures had understood—or that they would keep their word or be able to convey the terms of the deal to all the rest of Africa's crocodiles. She chose, however, to tell Angie that from that moment forward she had nothing to fear. She would not die in those big jaws, and with a little luck she would get her wish to die in a plane accident, she assured her.

Kosongo's wives, now happy widows, wanted to give their gold ornaments to Angie, but Brother Fernando intervened. He spread a blanket on the ground and asked the women to put their jewels in it. Then he tied up the four corners and dragged the bundle to Queen Nana-Asante.

"This gold and a pair of elephant tusks is all the wealth we have here in Ngoubé. You will know how to use it," he explained.

"What Kosongo gave me is mine!" Angie protested, clutching her bracelets.

Brother Fernando demolished her with one of his apocalyptic glances, and held out his hands. Grumbling, Angie removed the bracelets and handed over the ones she already wore. He made her promise in addition that she would leave him the radio in her plane, so they could communicate, and that she would make a flight every two weeks, at her expense, to supply the village with essentials. In the beginning she would have to drop them from the air, until they could clear a bit of jungle for a landing field. Given the terrain, that would not be easy.

Nana-Asante agreed that Brother Fernando could stay in Ngoubé and set up his mission and his school, as long as they agreed on one premise. Just as people had to learn to live in peace, so, too, the gods. There was no reason why different gods and spirits could not share space in the human heart.

EPILOGUE

Two Years Later

◈

ALEXANDER COLD CAME TO THE door of his grandmother's apartment in New York carrying a bottle of vodka for her and a bouquet of tulips for Nadia. She had told him that at her graduation she was not going to wear flowers on her wrist or bodice, like all the other girls. She thought corsages were tacky. A light breeze relieved the May heat slightly, but even so, the tulips were fainting. Alex thought he would never get used to the climate of this city, and was happy he didn't have to. He was attending university in Berkeley and, if his plans worked out, he would get his medical degree in California. Nadia accused him of being a little too comfortable. "I don't know how you're going to practice medicine in the poorest corners of the earth if you don't learn to get along without your mother's spaghetti and your surfboard," she teased him. Alexander had spent months convincing her of the advantages of having her study at his university, and finally had succeeded. In September she would be in California, and he wouldn't have to cross the continent to see her.

Nadia opened the door, and Alexander just stood there with red ears and the drooping tulips, not knowing what to say. They hadn't seen each other in six months, and the young woman who appeared in the doorway was a stranger. For a microsecond he wondered if he was at the wrong door, but his doubts dissipated when Borobá leaped on him to greet him with effusive hugs and nips. He heard his grandmother calling from the back of the apartment.

"It's me, Kate," he replied, still a little disoriented.

Then Nadia smiled, and she was again the girl of old, the girl he knew and loved, wild and golden. They embraced, the tulips dropped to the floor, and he put one arm around her waist and lifted her up with a shout of joy as with the other hand he struggled to free himself from the monkey's grip. Kate Cold showed up at that moment, dragging her feet. She seized the bottle of vodka that he was about to drop and kicked the door shut.

"Have you seen how awful Nadia looks? You'd think she was the girlfriend of some mafioso," said Kate.

Alexander burst out laughing. "Tell us what you really think, Grandma."

"Do *not* call me that! She bought that dress behind

my back. Without asking me!" she exclaimed.

"I didn't know you were interested in fashion, Kate," commented Alexander, eyeing the shapeless shorts and parrot design T-shirt that were his grandmother's uniform.

Nadia was wearing high heels and a short, tightly fitting, strapless dress of black satin. It should be said in her favor that she did not appear to be in the least affected by Kate's opinion. She did a slow turn to show off the dress to Alexander. She looked very different from the girl he remembered, the one in khaki shorts, with feathers in her hair. He would have to get used to the change, he thought, though he hoped it wasn't permanent. He liked the old Eagle a lot. He didn't know how to behave before this new version of his friend.

"You'll have to go through the torture of going to the graduation with that scarecrow, Alexander," said his grandmother, waving toward Nadia. "Come in here; I want to show you something."

She led the two young people to the tiny, dusty office where she wrote. As always, it was crammed with books and documents. The walls were papered with photographs she'd taken in recent years. Alexander recognized the Indians of the Amazon posing for the Diamond Foundation; Dil Bahadur, Pema, and their baby in the Kingdom of the Golden Dragon; Brother Fernando at his mission in Ngoubé; Angie Ninderera on an elephant with Michael Mushaha; and many others. Kate had framed a 2002 cover of *International Geographic* that had won an important prize. The photograph, taken by Joel in a market in Africa, showed him with Nadia and Borobá, confronting an irate ostrich.

"Look, Alex. Here are your three published books," Kate said. "When I read your notes, I realized that you will never be a writer; you don't have an eye for details. That may not be a drawback in the practice of medicine—the world is full of incompetent doctors—but in literature it's deadly," Kate assured him.

"I don't have the eye, and I don't have the patience, Kate. That's why I gave you my notes. I knew you could write the books better than I could."

"I can do almost everything better than you, Alexander." She laughed, ruffling his hair.

Nadia and Alexander looked through the books, feeling a strange sadness because they contained everything that had happened to them during three marvelous years of travel and adventure. In the future they might never experience anything comparable to what they'd already lived, nothing as intense or as magical.

At least it was a consolation to know that they, their stories, and the lessons they had learned would live on in those pages. Thanks to what Alex's grandmother had written, they would never be forgotten. The memoirs of Eagle and Jaguar were there in *City of the Beasts*, *Kingdom of the Golden Dragon*, and *Forest of the Pygmies*.

More magical adventures from
Isabel Allende

City of the Beasts

Fifteen-year-old Alexander Cold sets off on an expedition to the dangerous, remote world of the Amazon. Drawing on the strength of the jaguar, the totemic animal he finds within himself, Alexander is led on a thrilling journey to the ultimate discovery.

HC 0-06-050918-X · PB 0-06-053503-2 · AU 0-06-051076-5
Spanish edition: PB 0-06-051032-3

Kingdom of the Golden Dragon

Alexander and Nadia are off on another adventure, this time heading to an exotic sovereignty in the Himalayas. Their task is to locate its fabled golden dragon—a sacred, priceless key to the kingdom—before a greedy entrepreneur finds it. With the aid of a sage Buddhist monk, his young royal disciple, and a fierce tribe of Yeti warriors, they face an extraordinary battle to save the kingdom.

HC 0-06-058942-6 · PB 0-06-058944-2 · AU 0-06-059759-3
Spanish edition: HC 0-06-059170-6 · PB 0-06-059171-4

HarperTrophy® rayo
An Imprint of HarperCollinsPublishers

www.harpercollinschildrens.com
Both titles available in Spanish and Audio editions.